from

daddy

AS NIGHT TURNED TO DAWN, a muscular figure could be seen running through the streets of Washington, D.C. With a polite "On your left," the figure blew past another early-morning runner, Sam Wilson. Puzzled, Sam muttered to himself, "It's called jogging, man, ease up."

Sam continued his run. Passing the Washington Monument, he heard "On your left" again. This time Sam tried to catch up, but the figure was just too fast! Exhausted, Sam lay down on the grass to catch his breath. After a moment, the figure approached and asked Sam if he needed a medic. Sam quipped, "I need a new set of lungs!" then looked up. To his surprise, he saw Steve Rogers, more famously known as Captain America, the Super-Soldier and First Avenger!

Sam introduced himself as a former soldier, just like Steve. But now he worked at the local Department of Veterans Affairs, helping soldiers cope with coming back from active duty. Steve thanked Sam for his service and told him that he was doing a very important job.

Before Sam could respond, S.H.I.E.L.D. agent Natasha Romanoff drove up in a slick sports car. She informed Steve that Nick Fury and S.H.I.E.L.D. needed him: there was a hostage situation in the Indian Ocean. Steve told Sam he'd see him around. Sam watched in awe as the one and only Captain America went off to save the day!

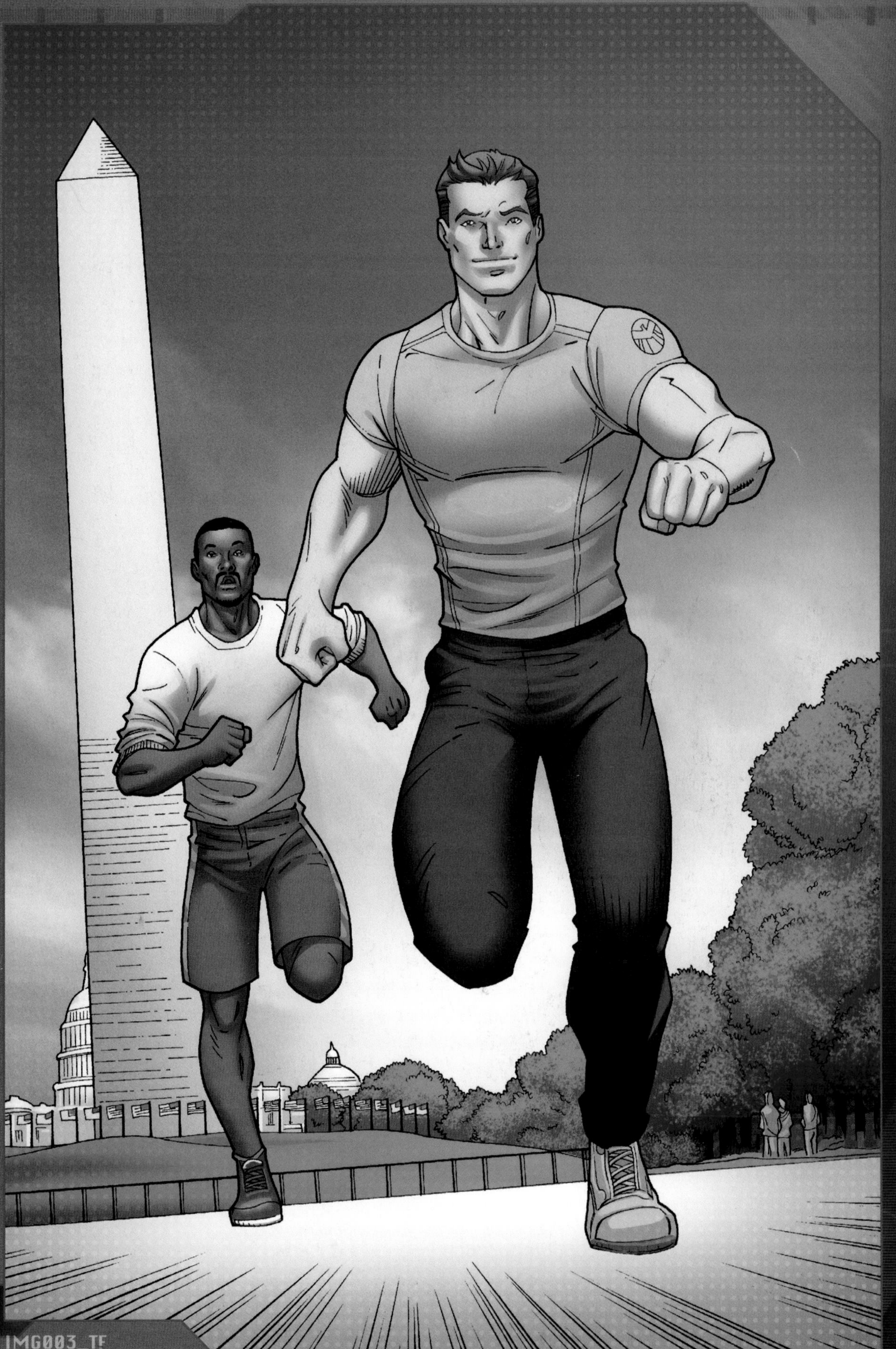
IMG003_TF

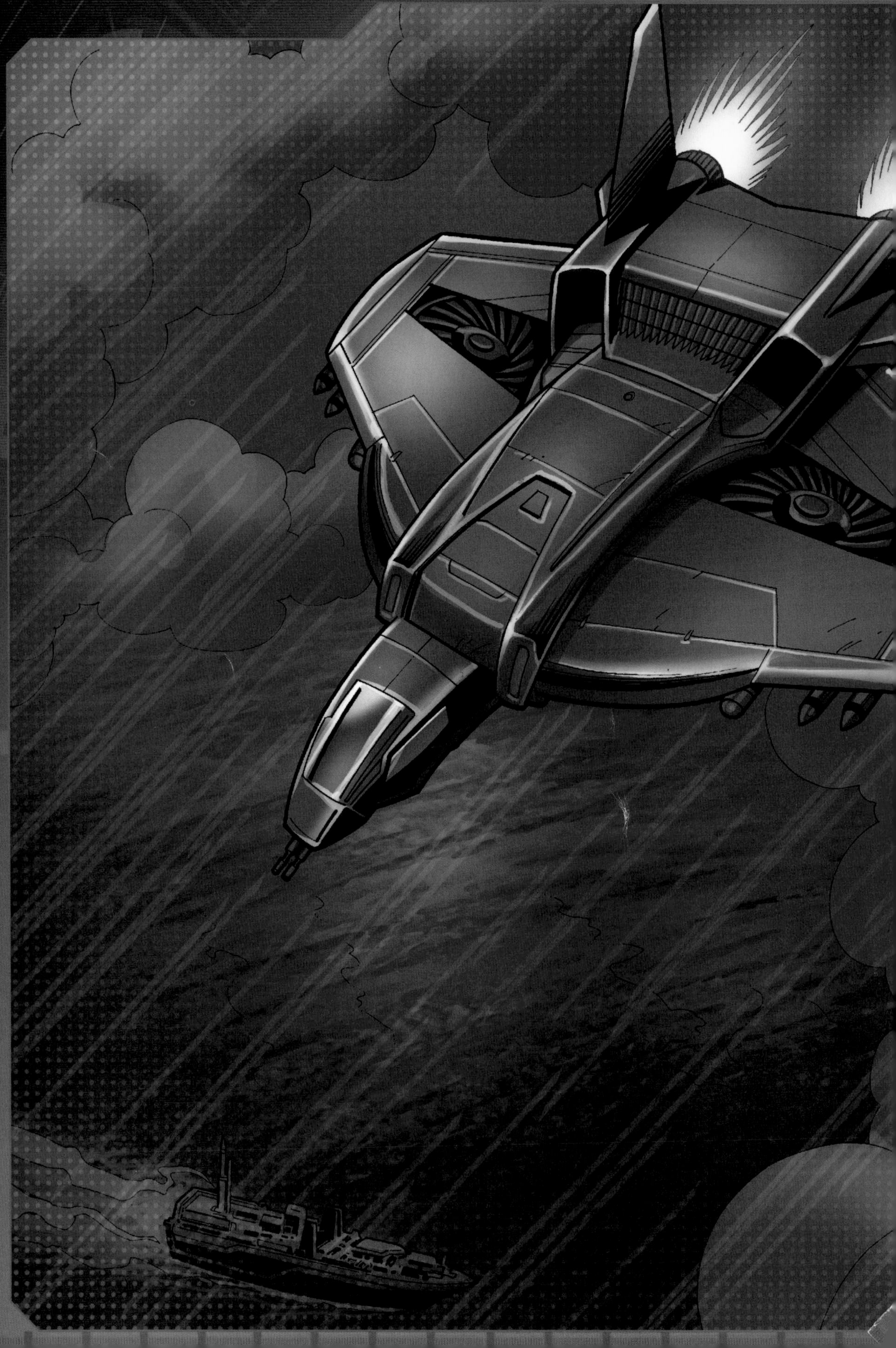

As S.H.I.E.L.D.'S hi-tech Quinjet swept through the clouds over Africa toward the Indian Ocean, Steve, in a stealth version of his Captain America uniform, and Natasha, geared up as super spy Black Widow, learned more about the hostage situation on S.H.I.E.L.D.'s huge ship, the *Lemurian Star*. S.T.R.I.K.E. team leader Brock Rumlow and his unit informed them that a dangerous man known as Georges Batroc had taken over the ship with a band of pirates and was holding the crew for a ransom of over a billion dollars!

A TRUE LEADER, Captain America gave the orders to the team: Black Widow would cut the engines so the boat wouldn't go anywhere; Rumlow and the S.T.R.I.K.E. team would find and rescue the hostages; and Cap would clear the ship's deck of pirates and find Batroc.

The jump door opened at the rear of the Quinjet and Cap dove out! One of the S.T.R.I.K.E. team members looked at Rumlow and asked, "Was he wearing a parachute?"

"No. No, he wasn't," replied Rumlow.

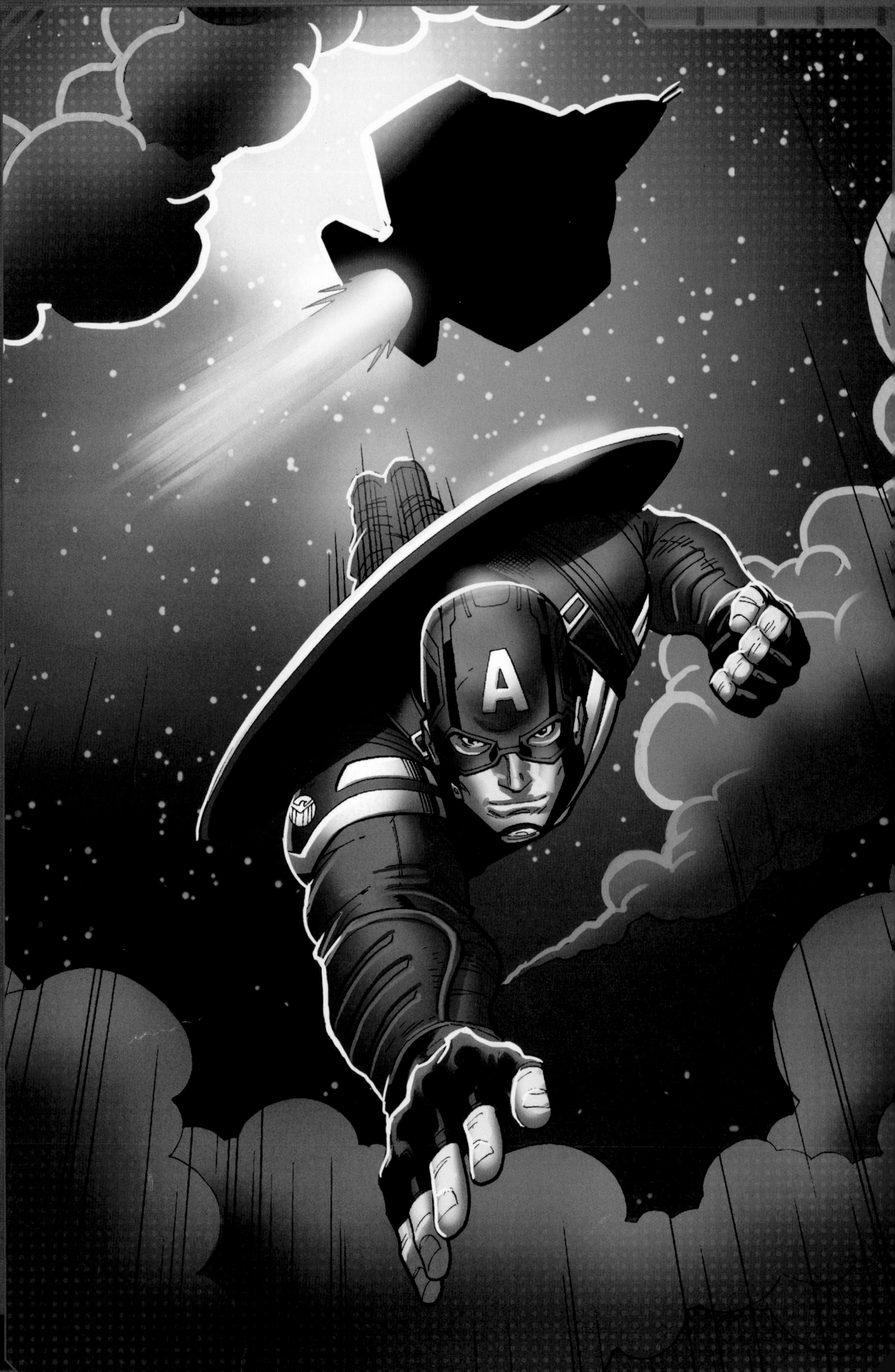

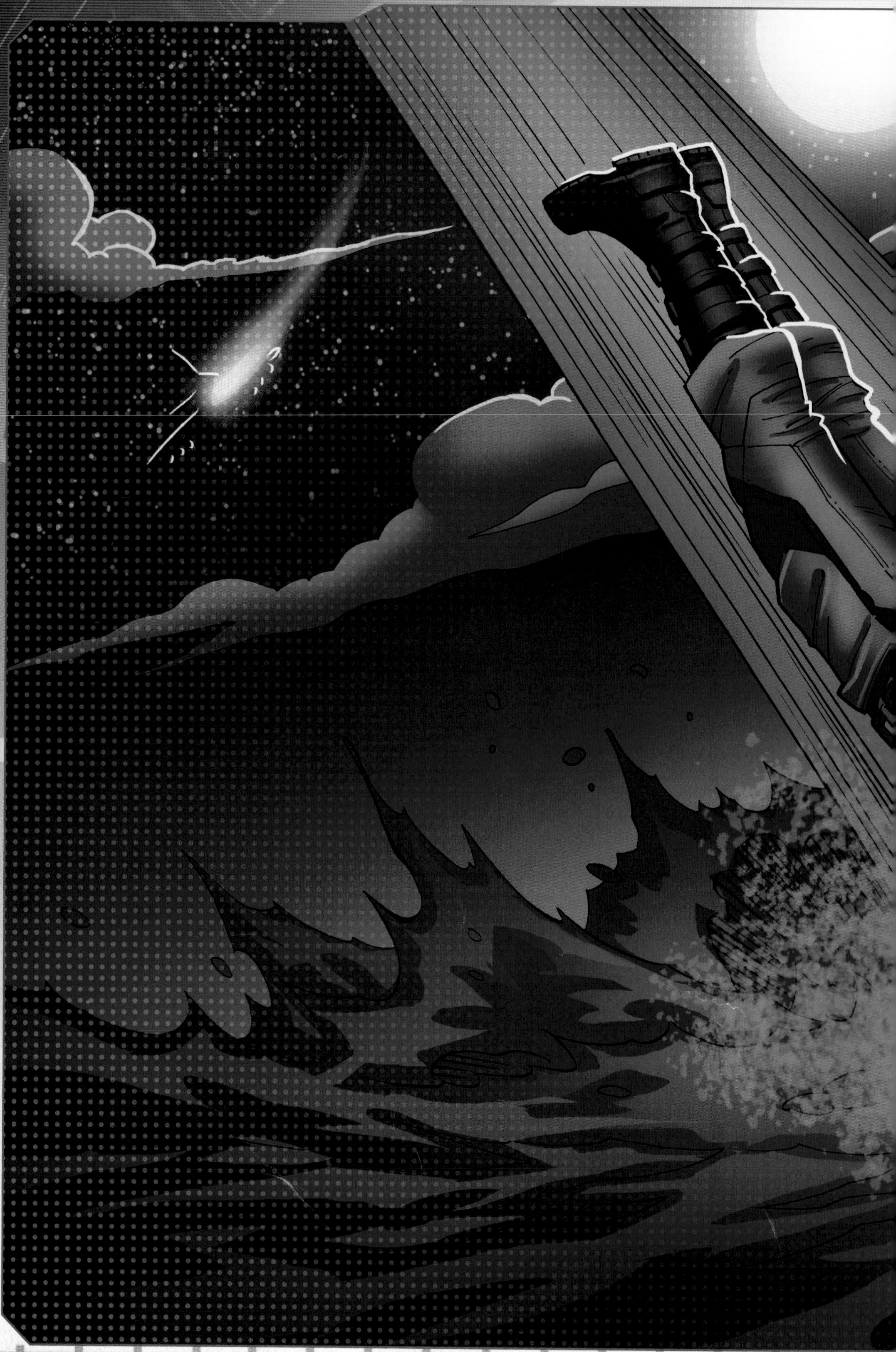

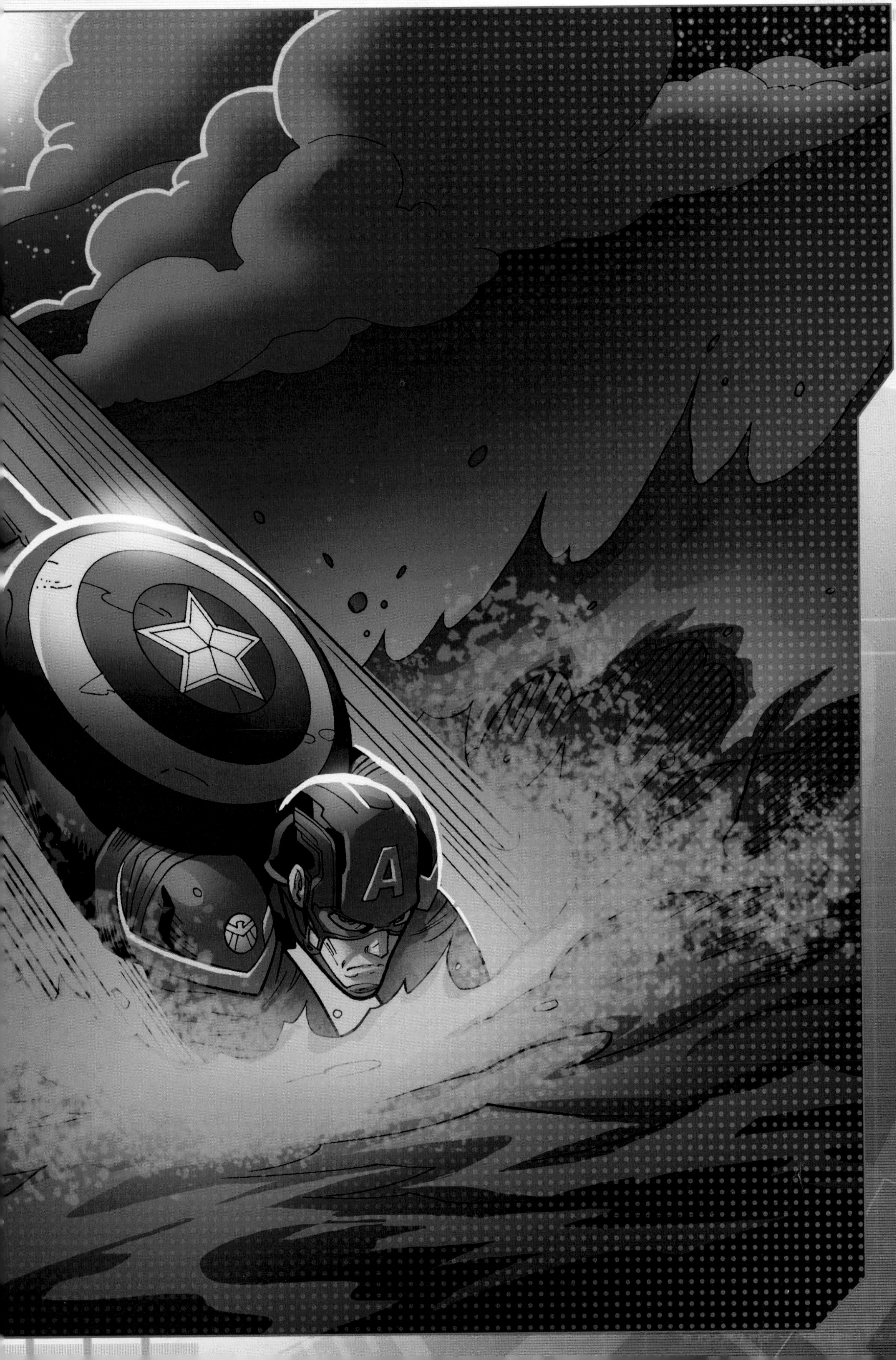

A DANGEROUS GROUP OF PIRATES PATROLLED THE SHIP'S DECK. From the dark water below came Captain America, stealthily pulling himself up onto the vessel. He silently knocked out the pirates and continued across the deck as, above him, Black Widow, Rumlow, and the S.T.R.I.K.E. team glided down in parachutes and quickly headed to fulfill their designated missions. It was then time for Cap to find Batroc.

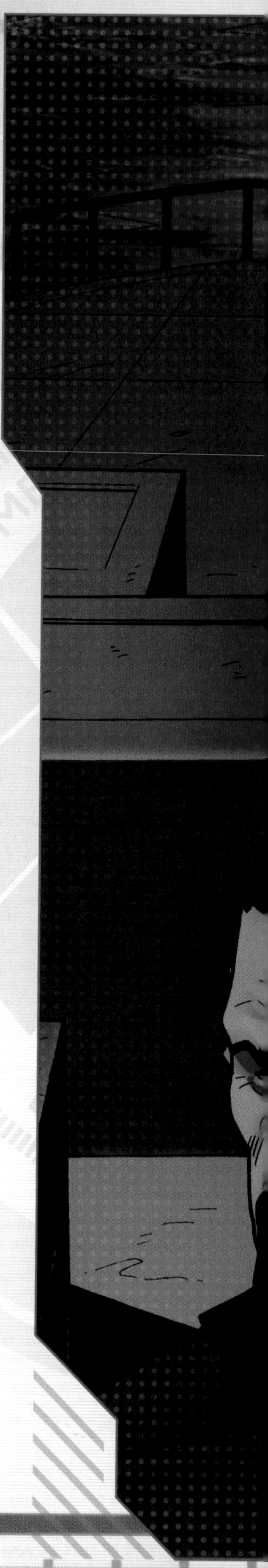

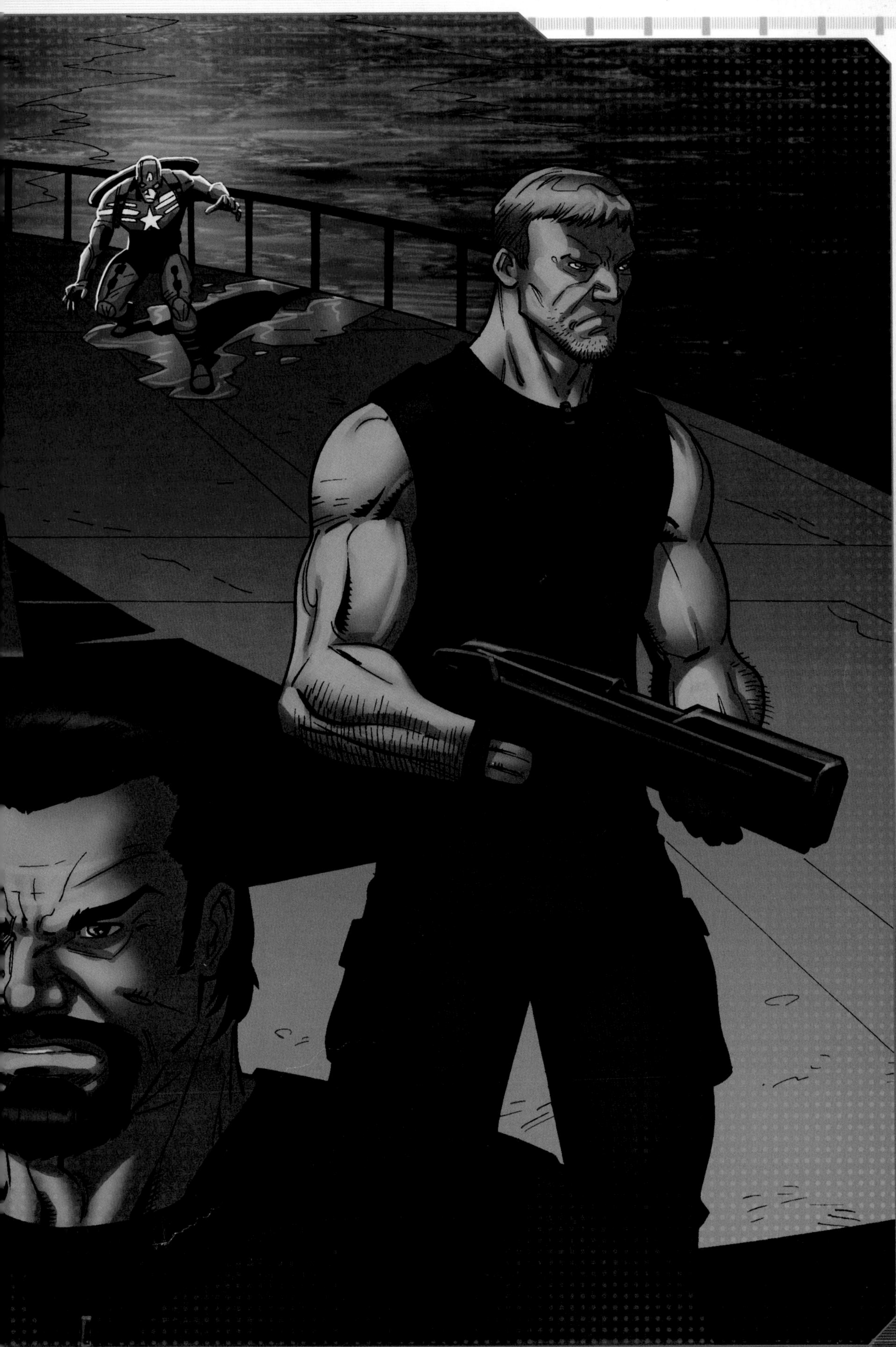

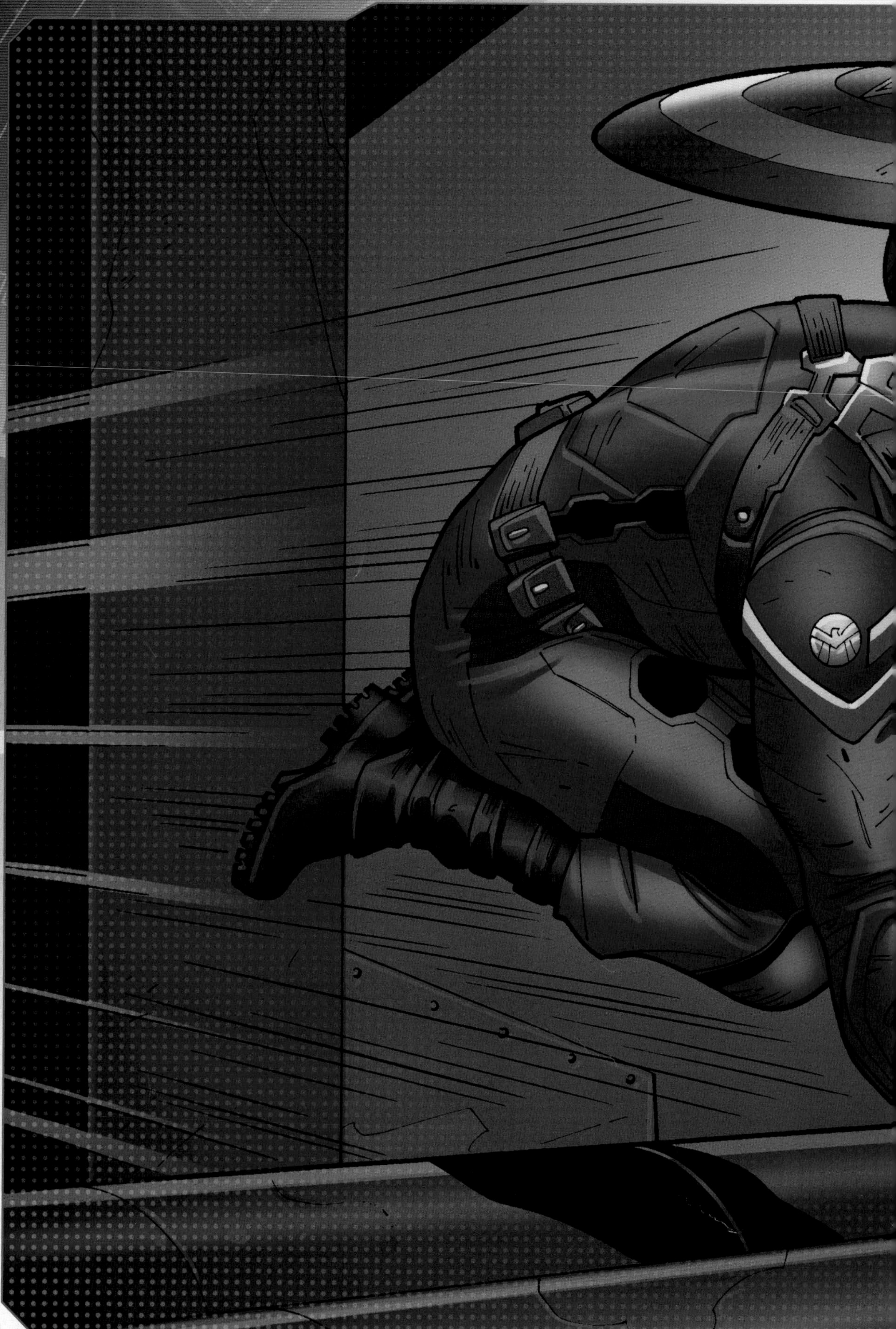

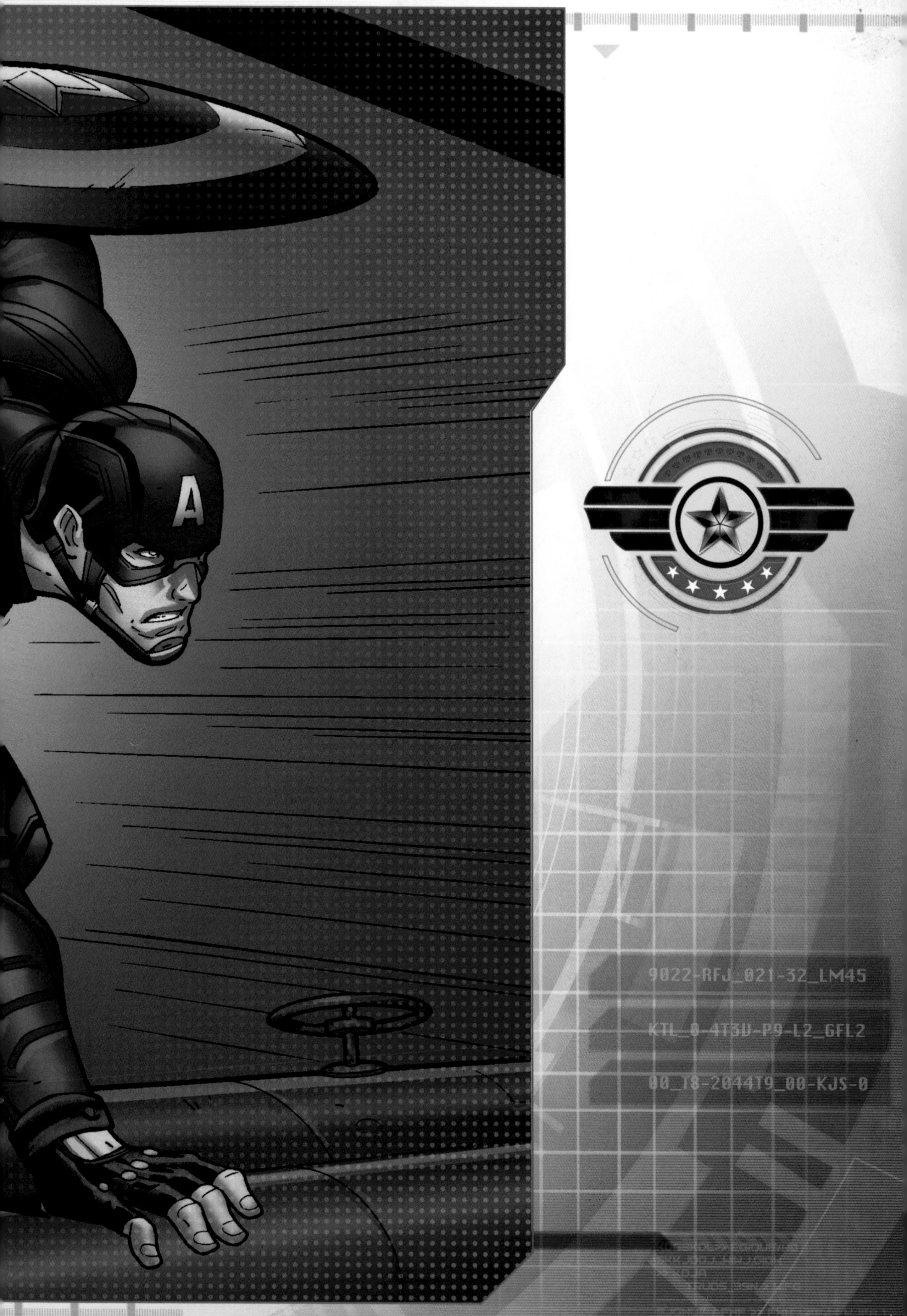
9022-RFJ_021-32_LM45
KTL_0-4T3U-P9-L2_GFL2
00_T8-2044T9_00-KJS-0

CAP EXPERTLY RACED ACROSS THE BOW OF THE SHIP, jumping, leaping, and diving over and under pipes and cargo bins. Along the way he took out pirate after pirate! He sprinted along the deck, sliding under a villain at full speed, flipping him over. The Super-Soldier turned a corner and ran into several more pirates. With a flurry of kicks and punches, Cap took them out with ease! He raced on, leaping down to the lower deck and dispatching a group of raiders in short order with his Vibranium shield.

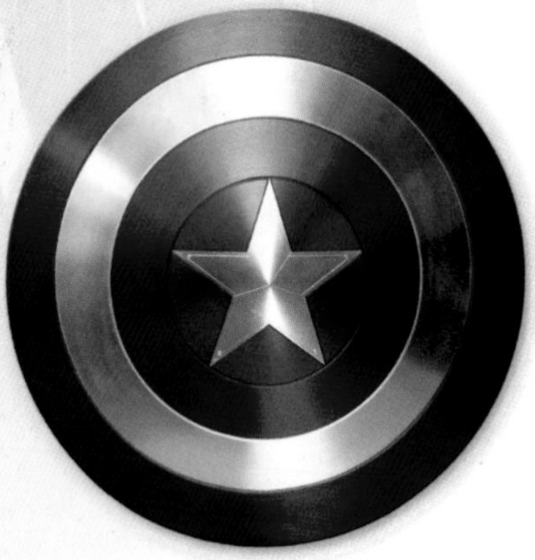

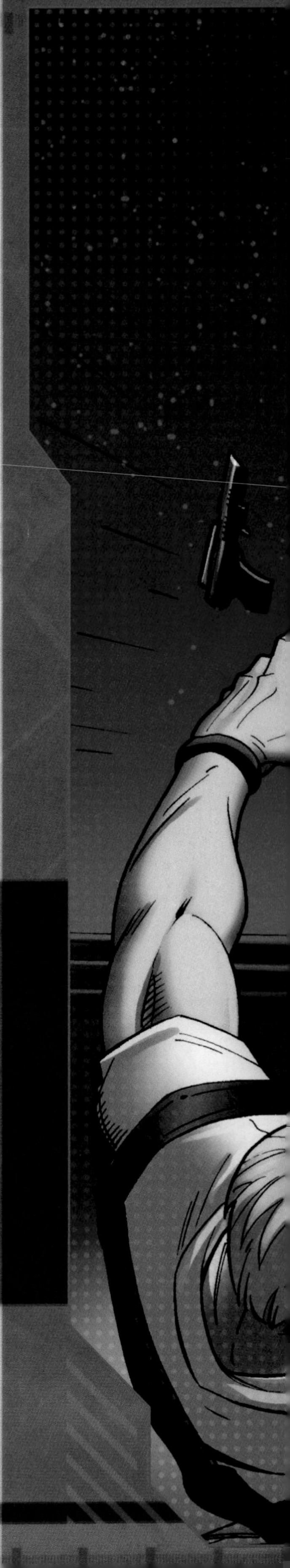

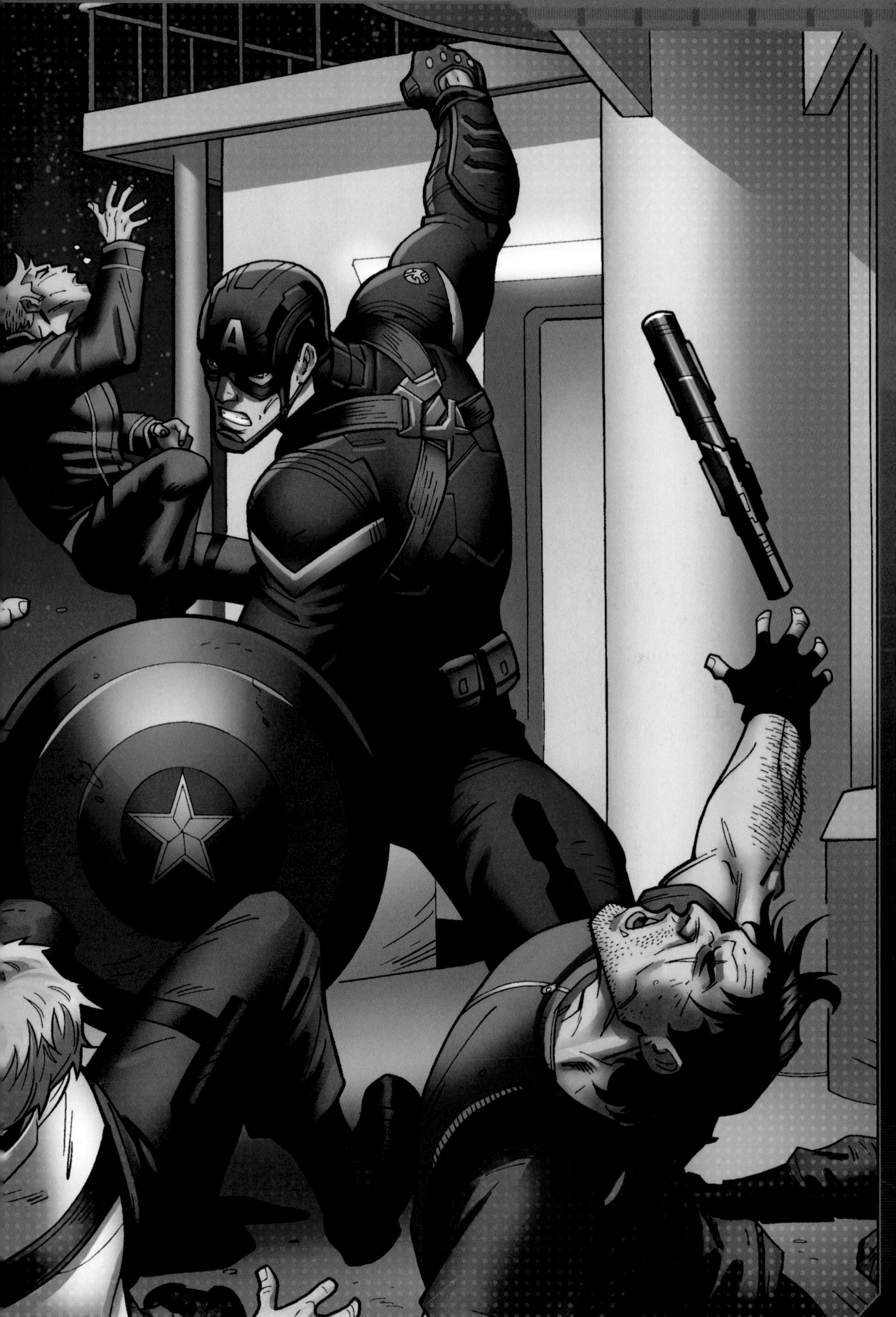

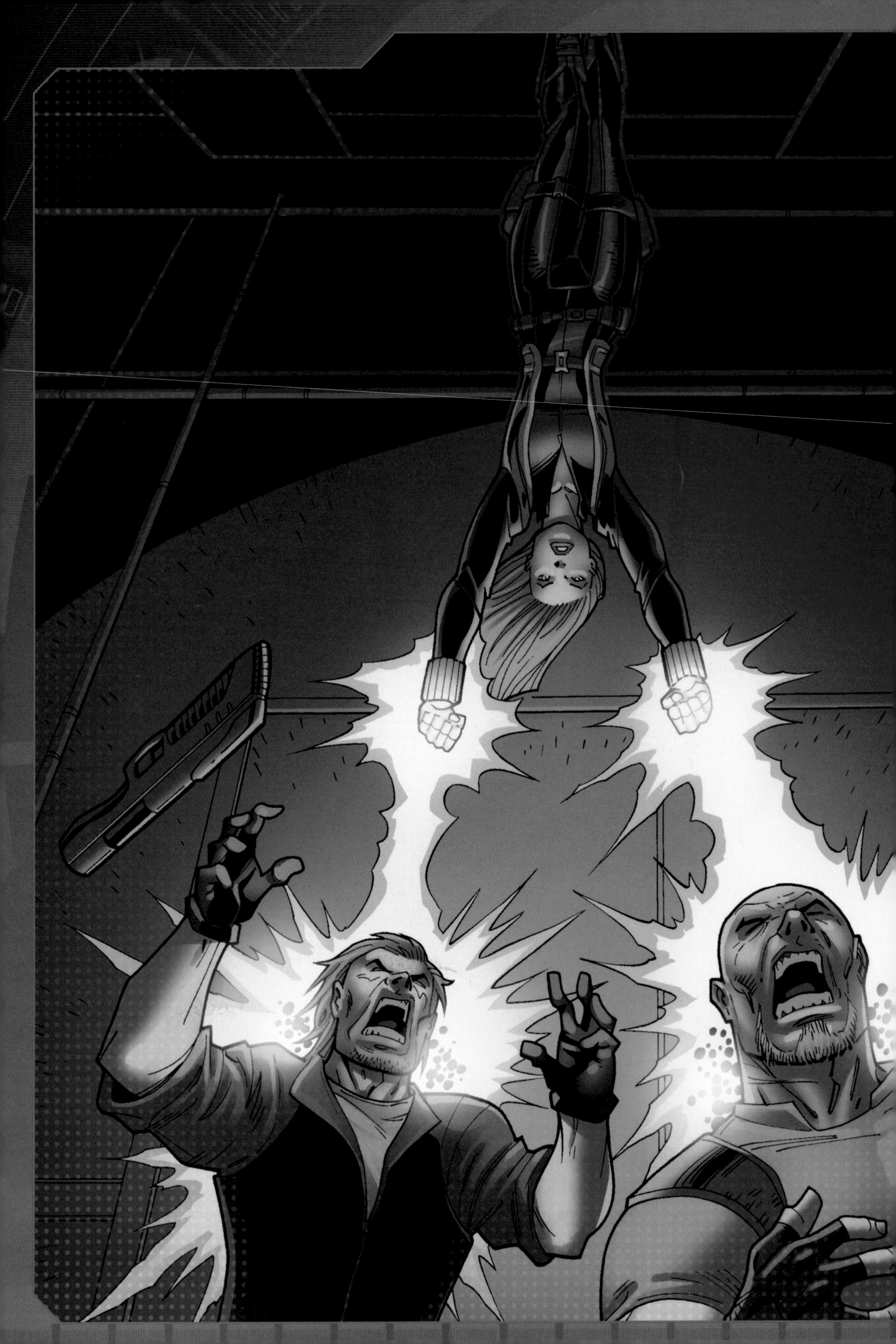

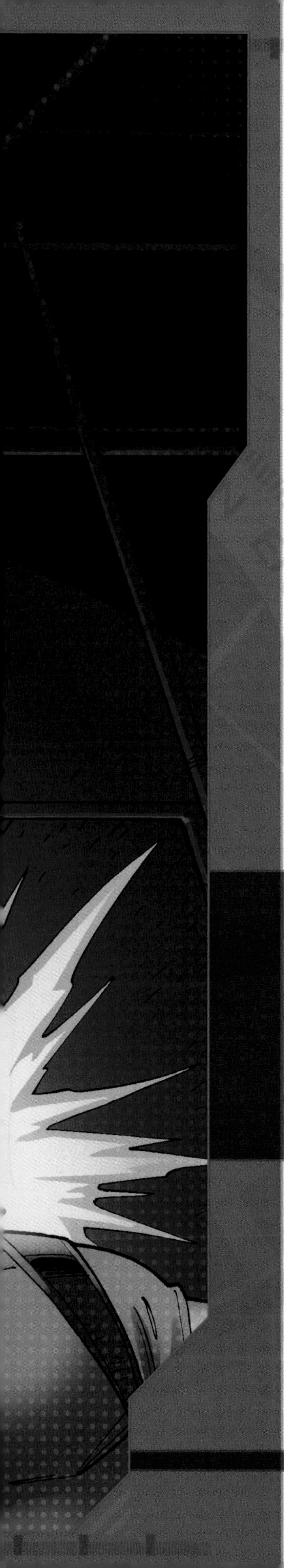

Outside the control room, the super spy Black Widow quietly descended from the ceiling to a floor beneath her and used her Widow's Bite bracelets to dispatch a group of thuggish pirates! Her "bites" delivered a small electric shock to her enemies, just enough to put them to sleep. Stunned, the goons dropped to the boat's deck. Black Widow flipped mid-air and landed silently on her feet. She smiled and raced off. Too easy, she thought.

DEEP WITHIN THE HULL OF THE *LEMURIAN STAR*, located inside a secret control room, Georges Batroc continued to make more demands to S.H.I.E.L.D. He gave a sinister smirk and nod to his men. If S.H.I.E.L.D. wanted the hostages, Batroc would get what he asked for.

Batroc was ready to fire up the engines to move the ship once the ransom came. But out of the corner of his eye, he saw Brock Rumlow and the S.T.R.I.K.E. team. They had reached the hostages! His plans were falling apart!

Furious, Batroc leaped over a railing to attack but was stopped by Captain America.

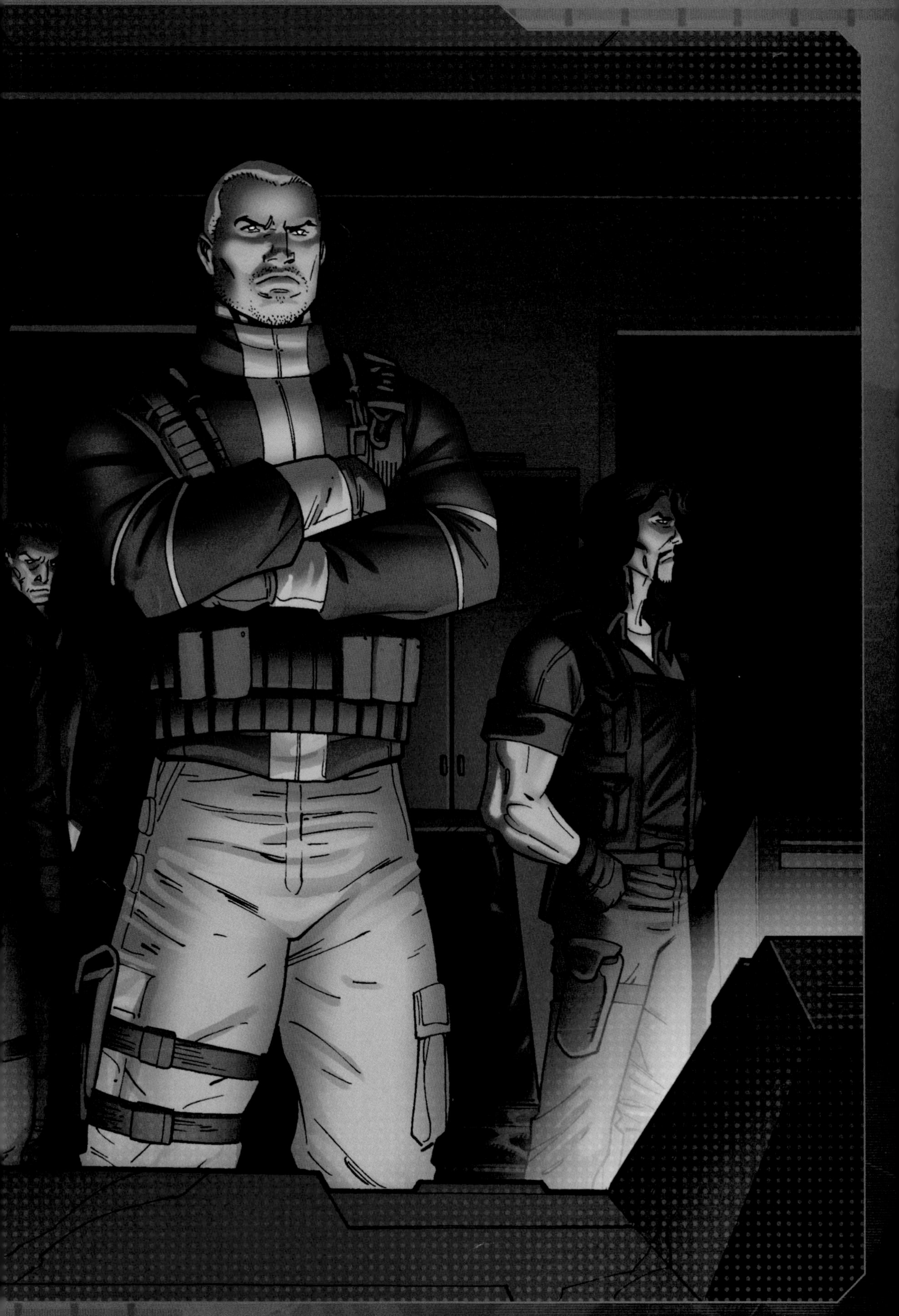

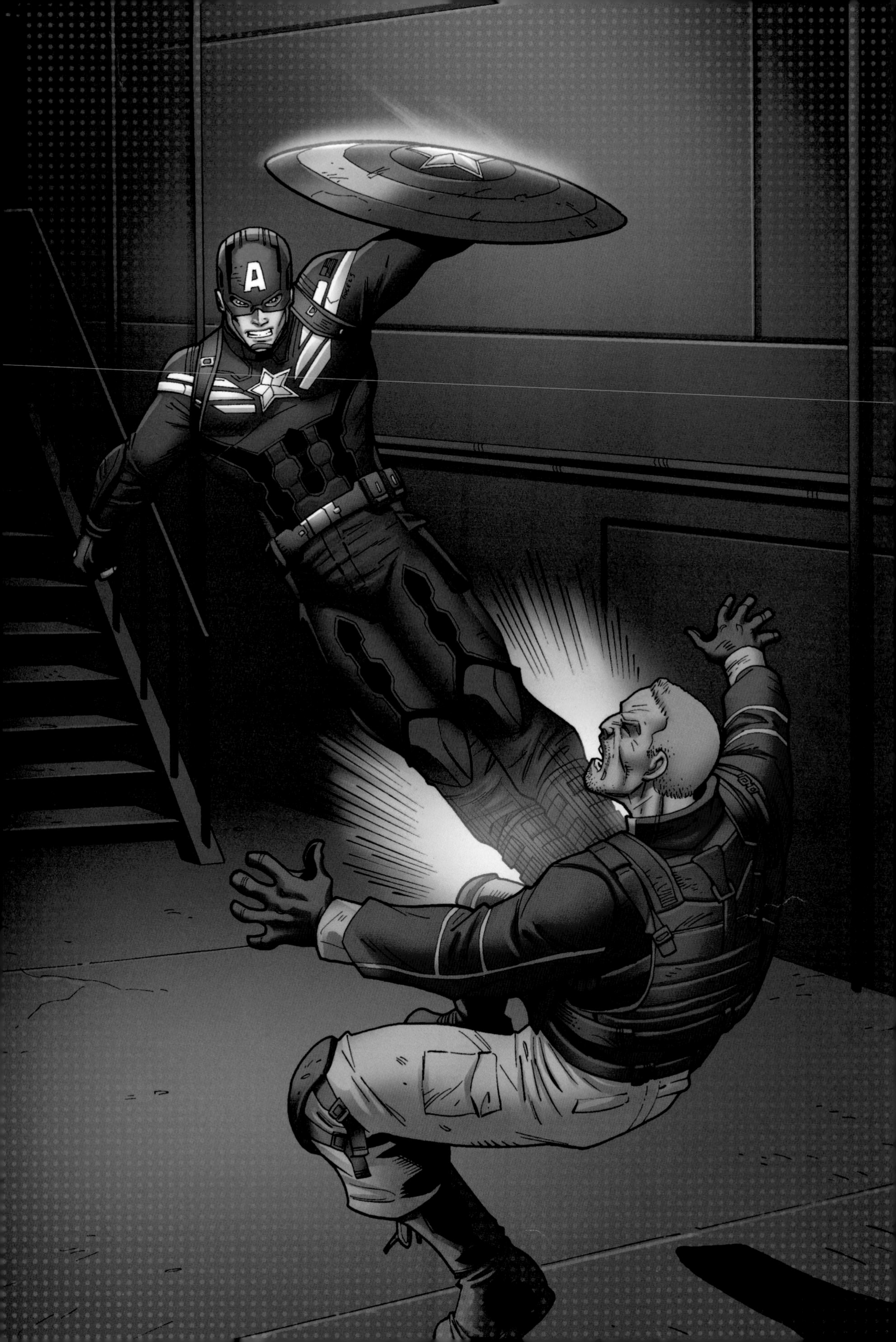

As Rumlow and the S.T.R.I.K.E. team rescued the hostages, Batroc attacked Cap with series of super kicks, knocking him back! Cap blocked the shots with his shield and regained his footing. This guy's quick, he thought as he lunged at Batroc, heaving the French fighter into a pipe.

Batroc instantly sprang up, renewing his attack.

Steve kept blocking the kicks and punches with his shield until Batroc yelled at him in French, "I thought you were more than just a shield!"

Surprisingly, Captain America responded in Batroc's native language. "Let's see," he said, strapping the shield onto his back. The two men squared off, trading blows. The fight was on!

Batroc pounced, his boot kicking Cap in the head. Pulling himself together from the Frenchman's strong series of kicks, Cap blocked and jabbed, matching Batroc's style.

Finally, Cap was able to overpower Batroc and slammed him through the control room's door, knocking him out.

Cap raced off down the hall when he heard movement in another room. He quietly opened the door, ready to attack a pirate if one was inside. But instead he found Black Widow at a bank of computers. She was filling a handheld data drive with info from the ship's mainframe. Steve asked Natasha what she was doing. Natasha said she was saving S.H.I.E.L.D.'s intel. It was her secret mission from Nick Fury.

Steve was frustrated. He thought the mission was to save the hostages. "That was your mission," Natasha replied. "And you handled it beautifully."

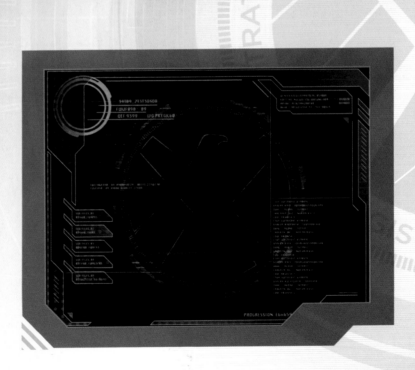

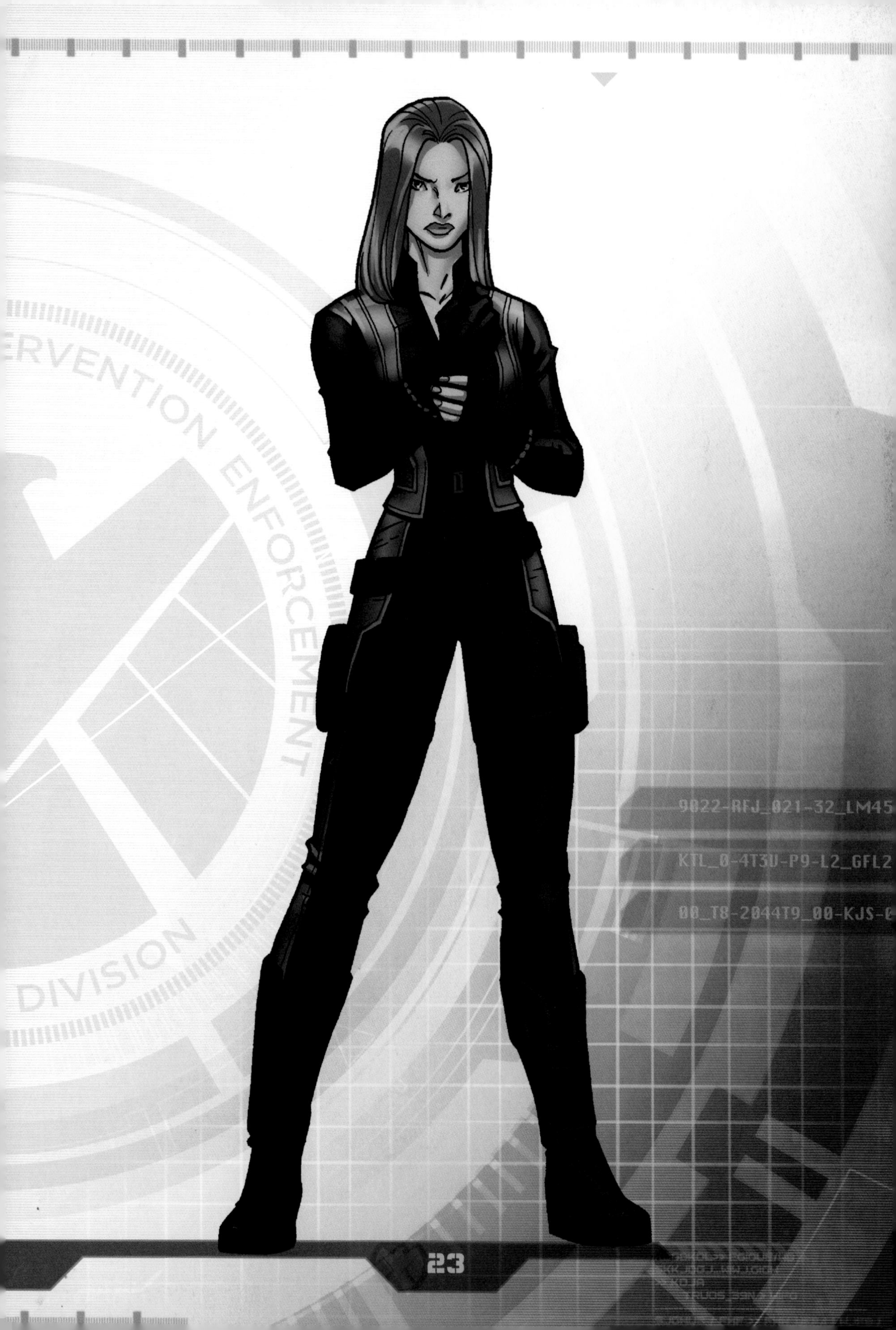
ERVENTION
ENFORCEMENT
DIVISION
9022-RFJ_021-32_LM45
KTL_0-4T3U-P9-L2_GFL2
00_T8-2044T9_00-KJS-C

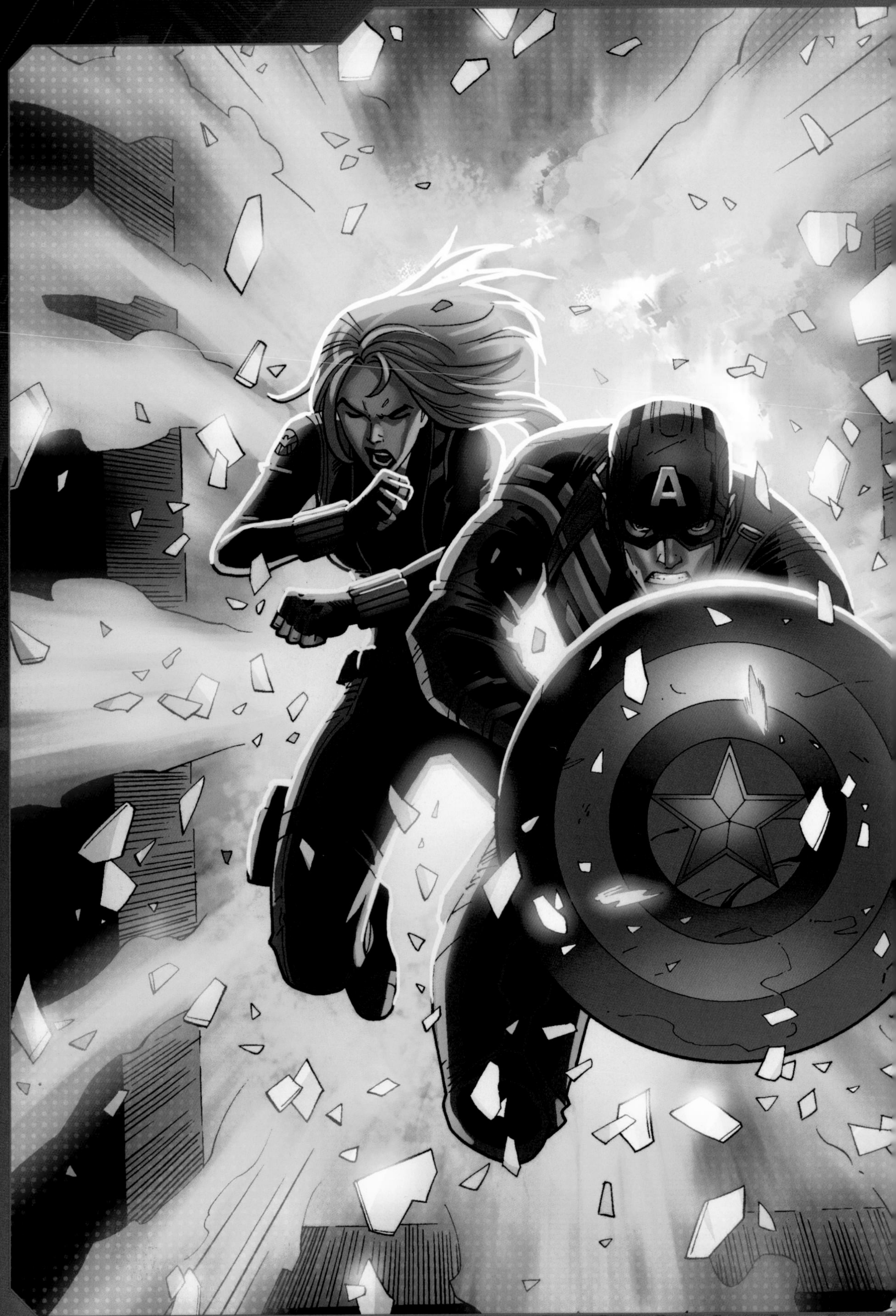

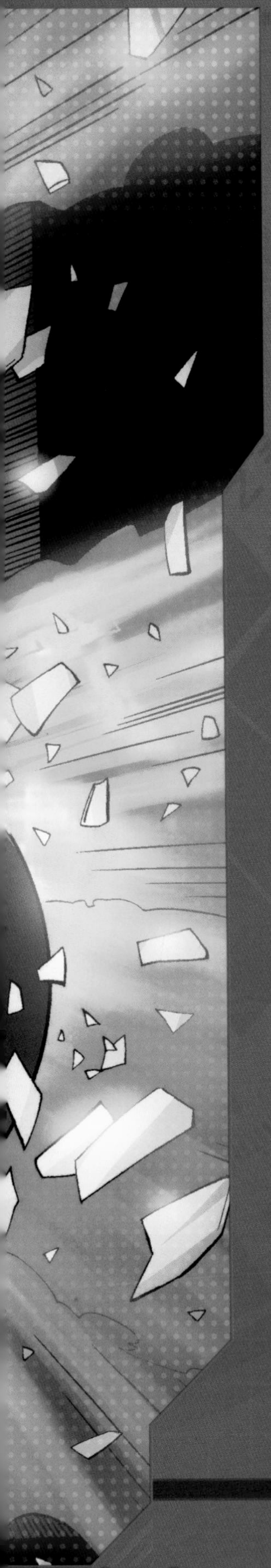

Before Cap could react he heard a TINK TINK! Suddenly, a hand grenade rolled across the floor. Steve whirled around to see Batroc escaping. Without thinking, both Captain America and Black Widow jumped through a window as a huge explosion rang out behind them!

KRAKOOM!!!!!

CAP AND BLACK WIDOW brushed off the dust and debris from the explosion and raced upstairs to the main deck where a group of helicopters whirled above them.

Rumlow and the S.T.R.I.K.E. team escorted the relieved hostages onto a waiting chopper. Even though Batroc mysteriously got away, at least the hostages are safe, Cap thought as he helped them aboard the rescue chopper. Black Widow called the circling Quinjet back to the *Lemurian Star* and the S.H.I.E.L.D. agents boarded it and headed back to base. Mission complete.

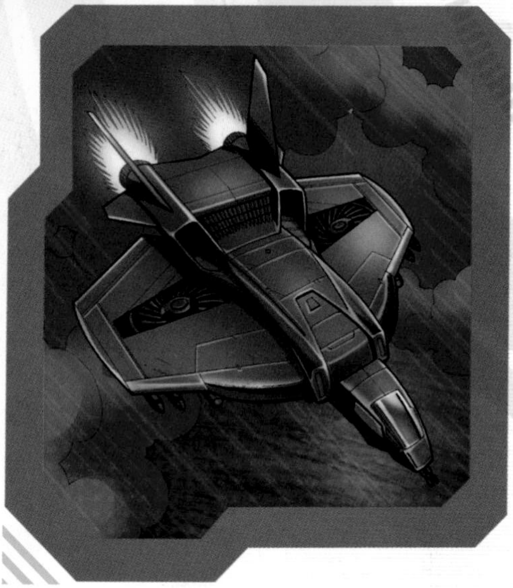

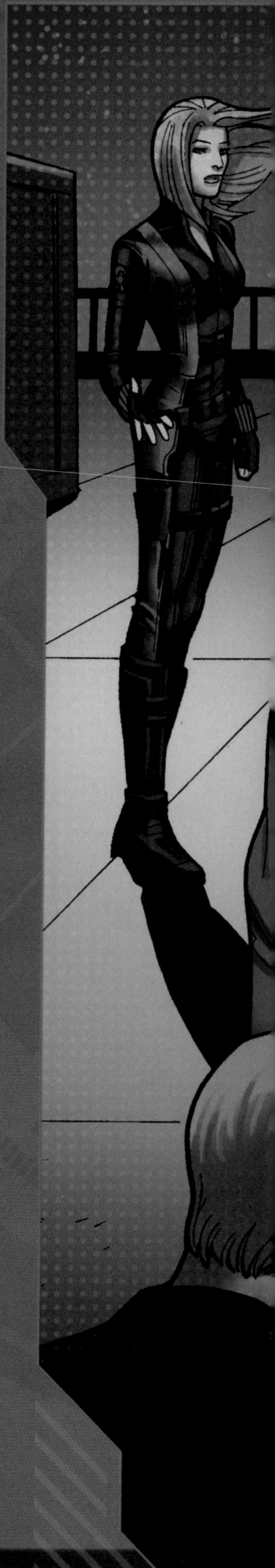

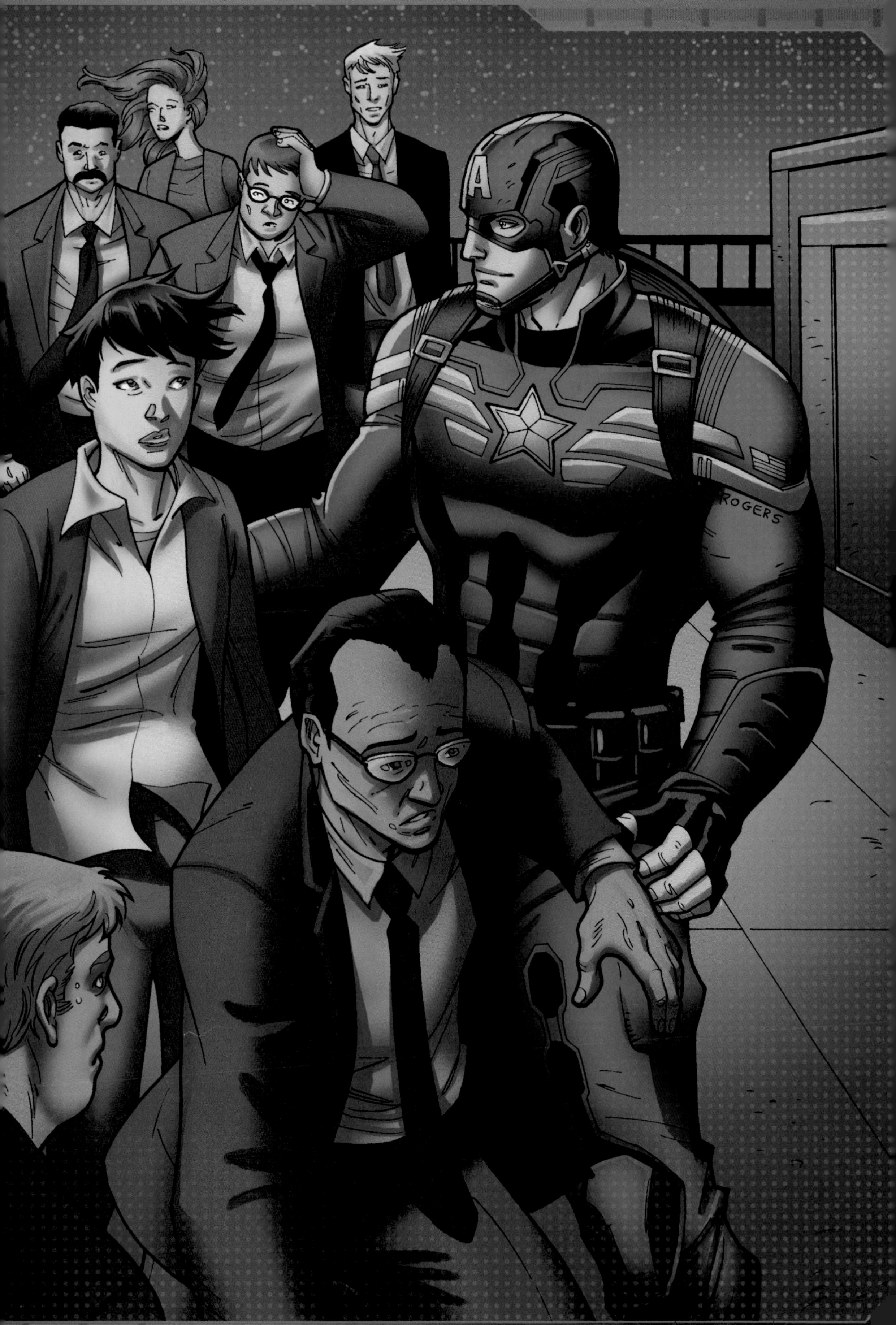
ROGERS

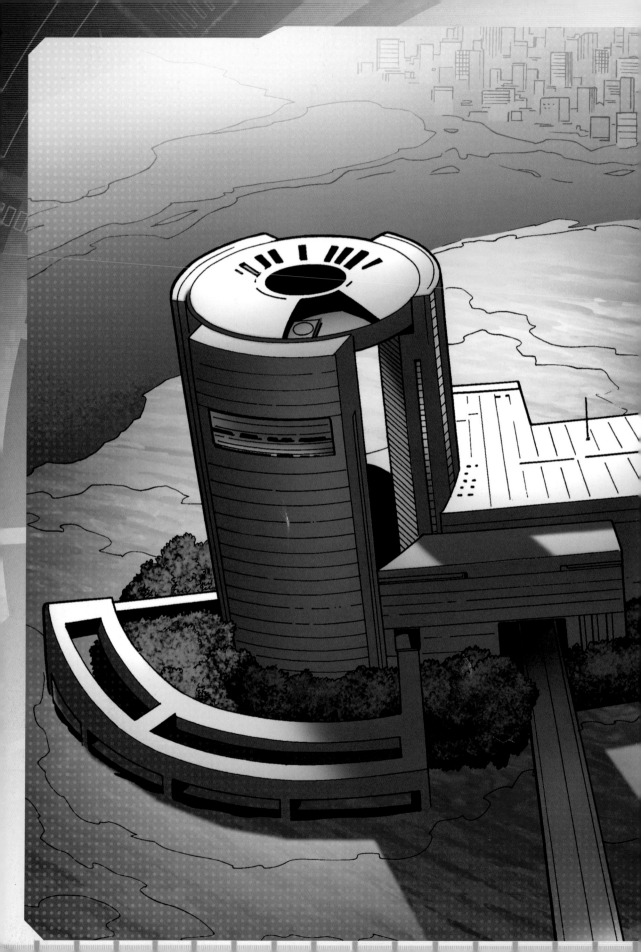

AT THE TRISKELION, S.H.I.E.L.D.'s massive Washington, D.C., headquarters, Steve was speaking to Nick Fury.

"You just can't stop yourself from lying, can you?" he pointedly asked.

The Director of S.H.I.E.L.D. was trying to make it clear that he hadn't lied to Steve, and that Agent Romanoff just had a different mission from his. Steve felt that Nick should have shared this information with him. "Soldiers trust one another. That's what makes an army," Steve flatly stated.

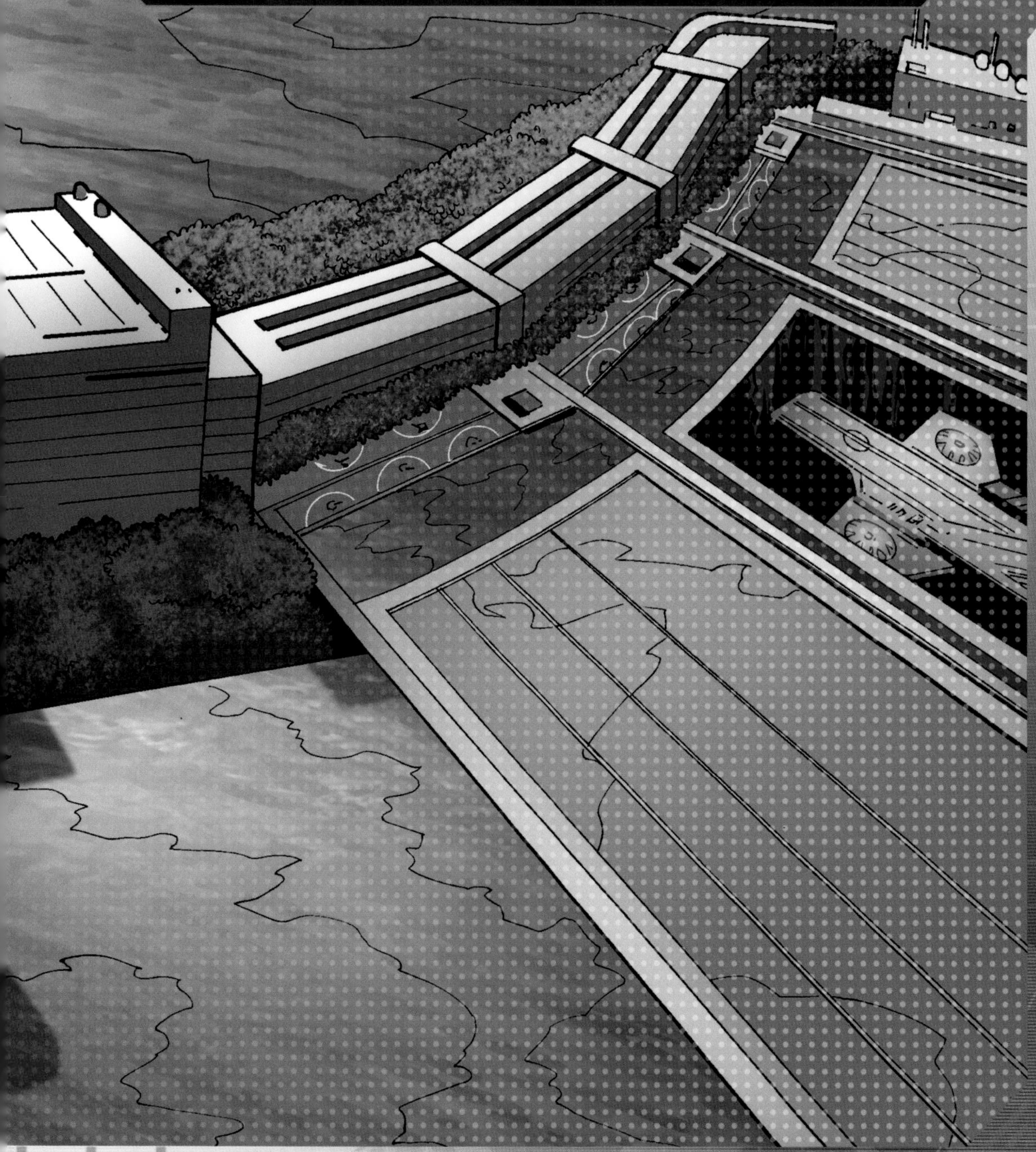

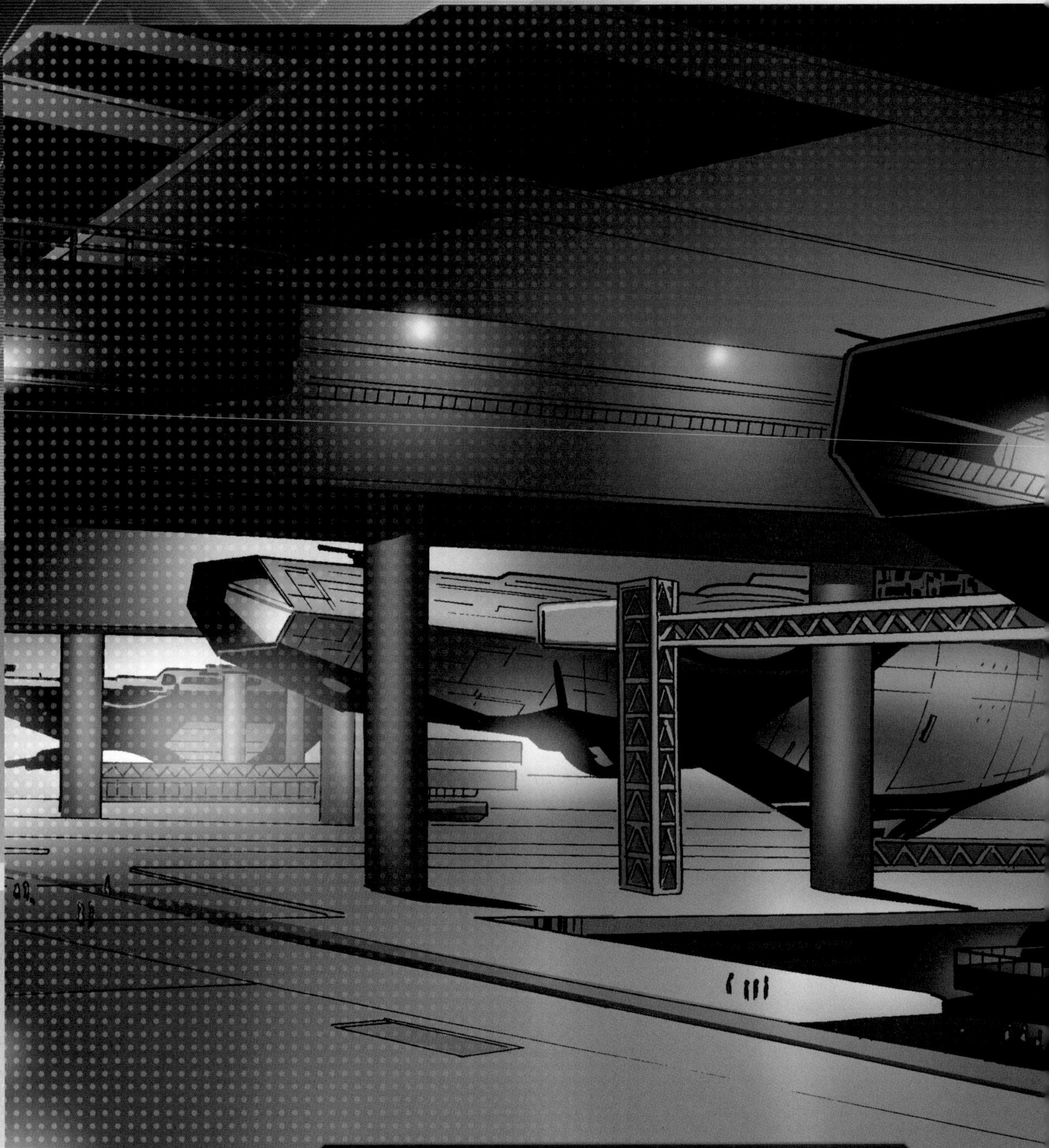

To show Steve how much he trusted him, Fury took him into an elevator. He pressed a button that shot them down to Insight Bay, an area even Captain America didn't have clearance for. Steve stepped out of the elevator, stunned at what he saw.

It was three brand-new Helicarriers, sleeker and more menacing than the old one, which was being dismantled nearby.

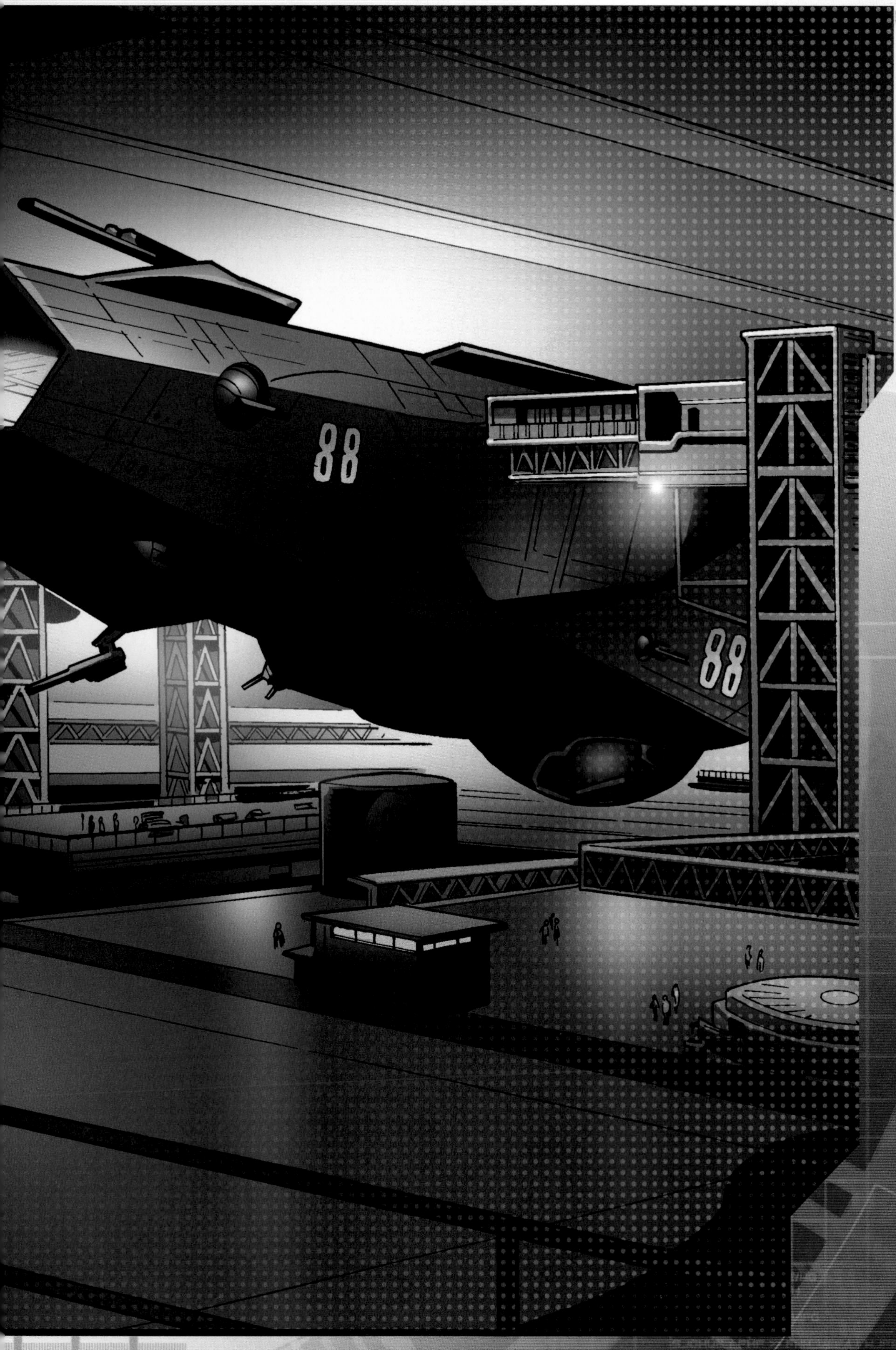
88
88

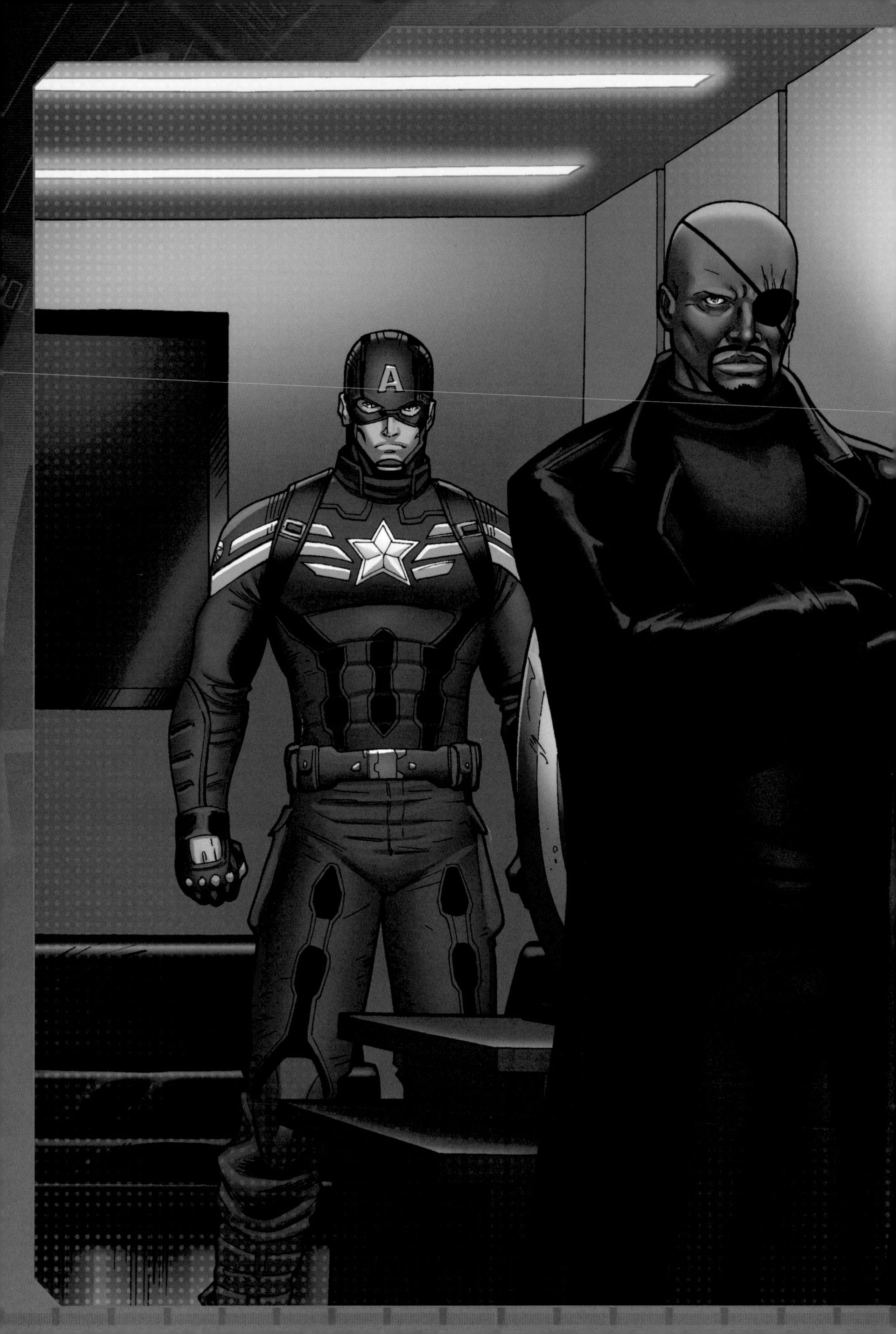

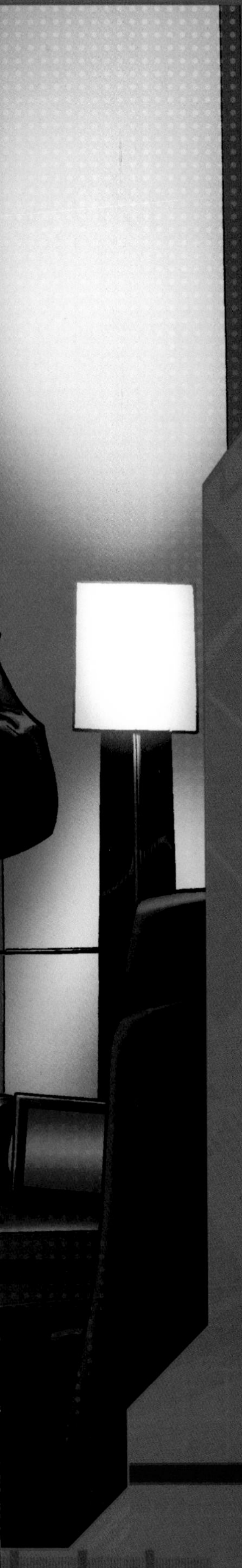

Fury explained that this was Project Insight, which had the purpose of launching the new Helicarriers into continuous suborbital flight, courtesy of the new repulsor engines suggested by Tony Stark, also known as Iron Man.

Fury and Steve walked beneath the new Helicarriers. Bristling out of a huge panel in the hull were thousands of individual needlelike weapons.

Steve was impressed but wary. What exactly did this all mean?

Back in his office, Fury explained that after the events involving the Chitauri and Loki attacking New York City and the Avengers coming to save the day, he and the World Security Council agreed that they needed to get ahead of the curve. And the only way to do that was to neutralize threats before they even started. The unibeam located at the front of the Helicarrier would be capable of eliminating a thousand individual targets per minute and the tech would be able to read a terrorist's DNA.

Steve felt uneasy about what the Helicarriers would be used for. After all, he'd joined S.H.I.E.L.D. to protect people, not threaten them.

"S.H.I.E.L.D. takes the world as it is, not as we'd like it to be," Fury explained.

Steve Rogers left, still frustrated about what he had just learned.

Holding the data drive Natasha had given him, Fury watched from his window as Steve peeled out on his motorcycle. Nick knew someone had gone to great lengths to try to steal secret information from S.H.I.E.L.D. and wondered if Batroc's hostage situation was a distraction for something else.

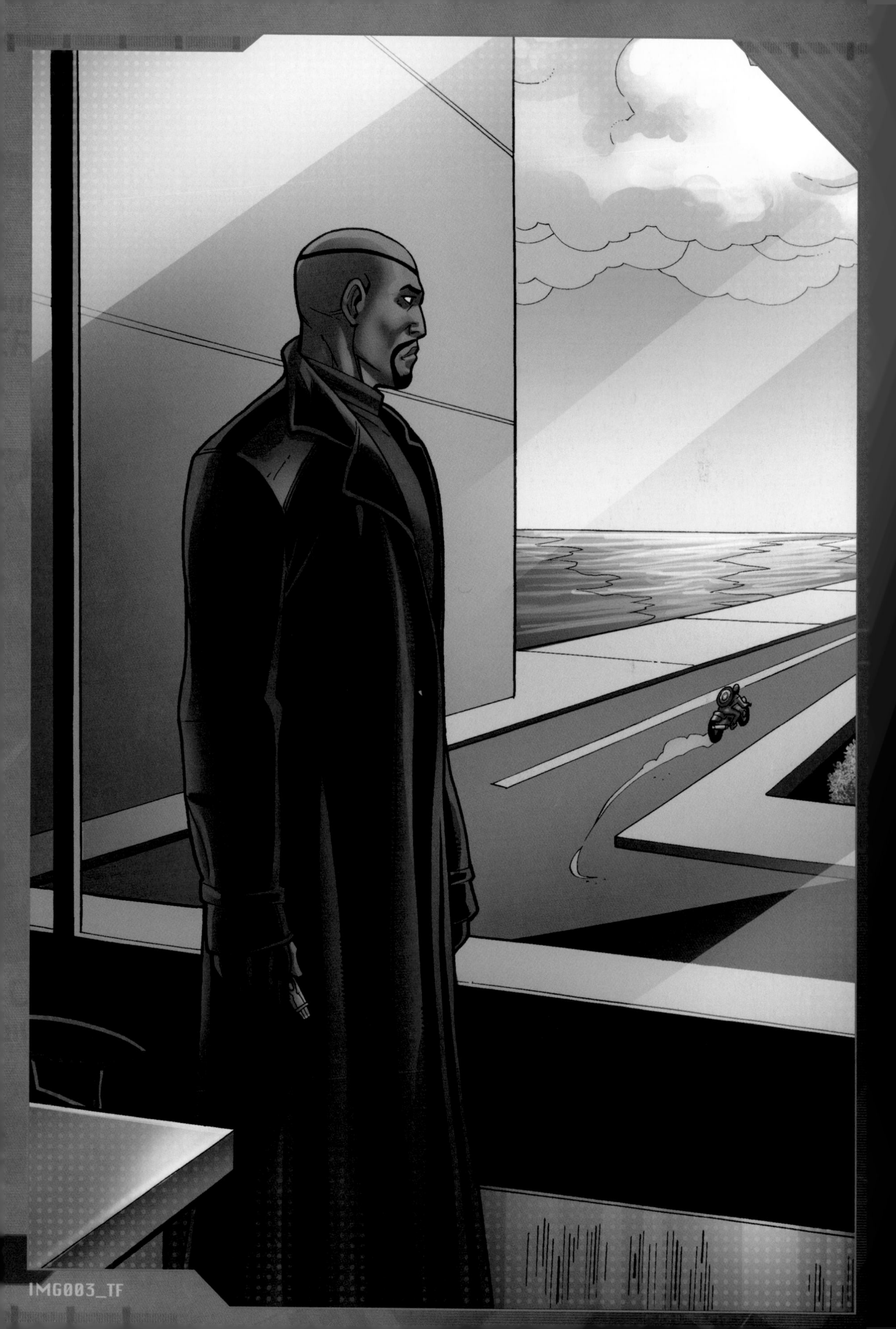
IMG003_TF

Tourists crowded the Captain America wing of a Washington, D.C., museum. Cap's theme song from the 1940s, "The Star-Spangled Man," floated into the vast hall through hidden speakers. A young child stood in front of a huge mural depicting Cap saluting. The child saluted right back just as Steve Rogers slunk past, hoping he wouldn't be noticed.

Giggling kids measured their height against "Skinny Steve," marveling at how small he had been before being chosen to receive the Super-Soldier Serum. One of the giggling kids noticed the real-life Captain America standing right behind him! Steve smiled and raised his finger to his lips. Shhh…

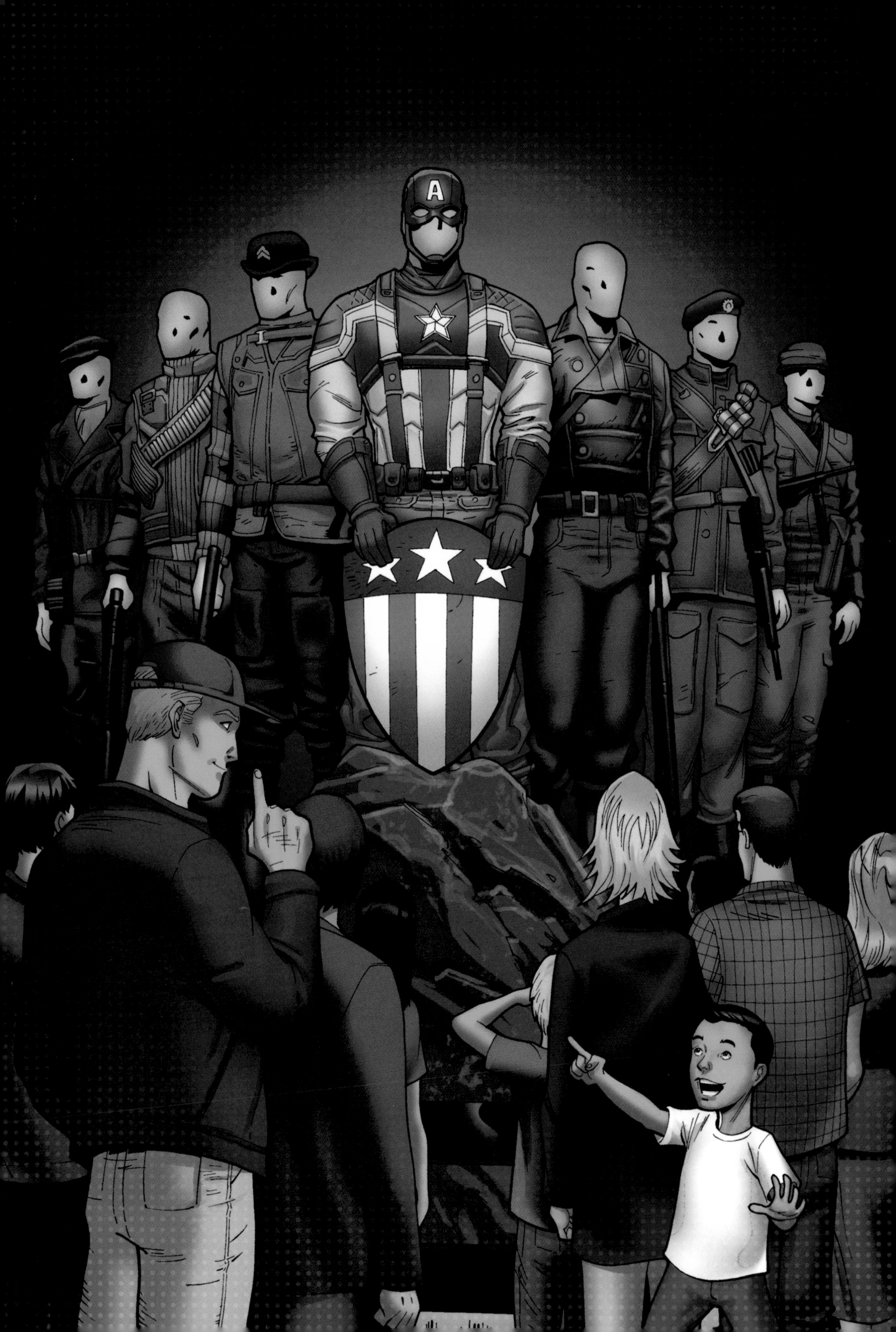

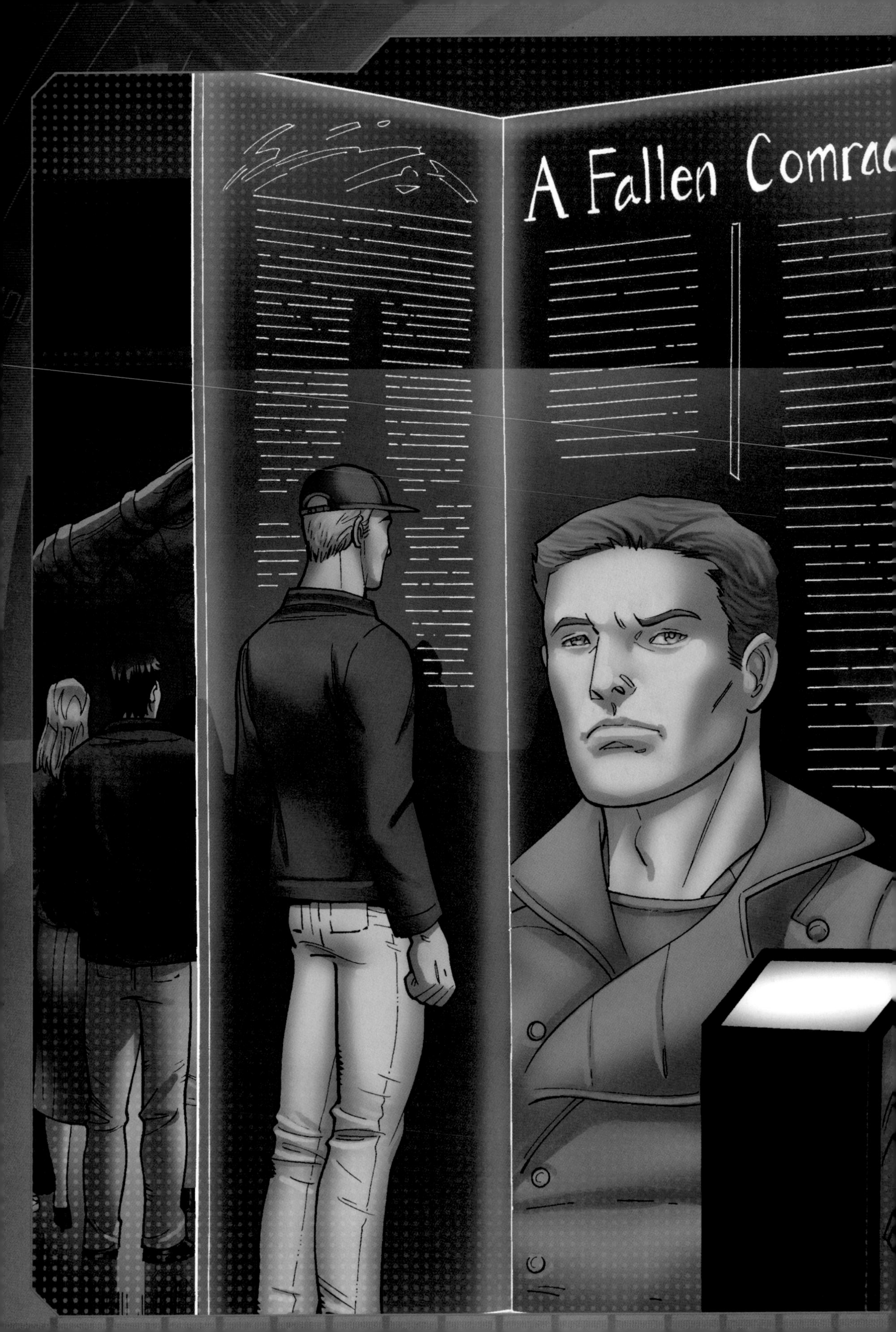
A Fallen Comrad

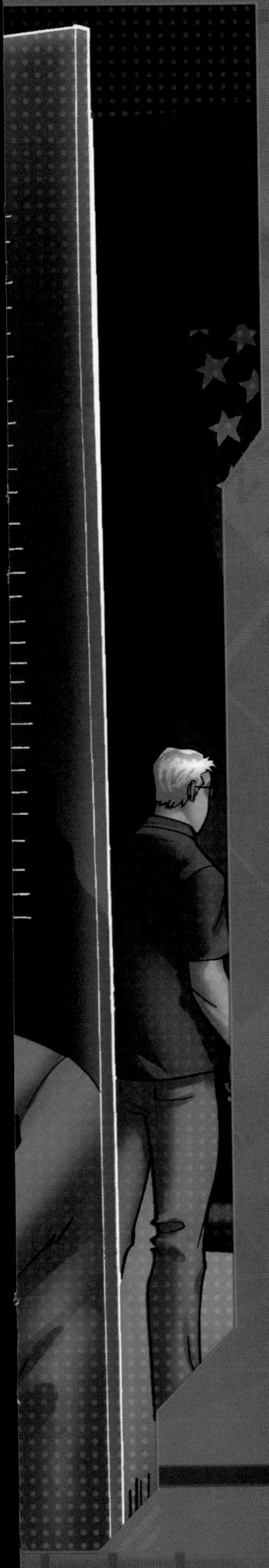

Steve walked past a display showing a Captain America mannequin in his World War II outfit leading the Howling Commandos into action. He then stopped at a somber exhibit. It was a picture of a smiling, skinny Steve and James "Bucky" Barnes, his best friend and comrade-in-arms. Steve remembered how inseparable they had been, both in the schoolyard and on the battlefield.

Bucky had given his life in service to his country, and even though Steve was proud of him, he was sad to have lost his best friend while battling the Red Skull. He came here to remember the good times they had shared.

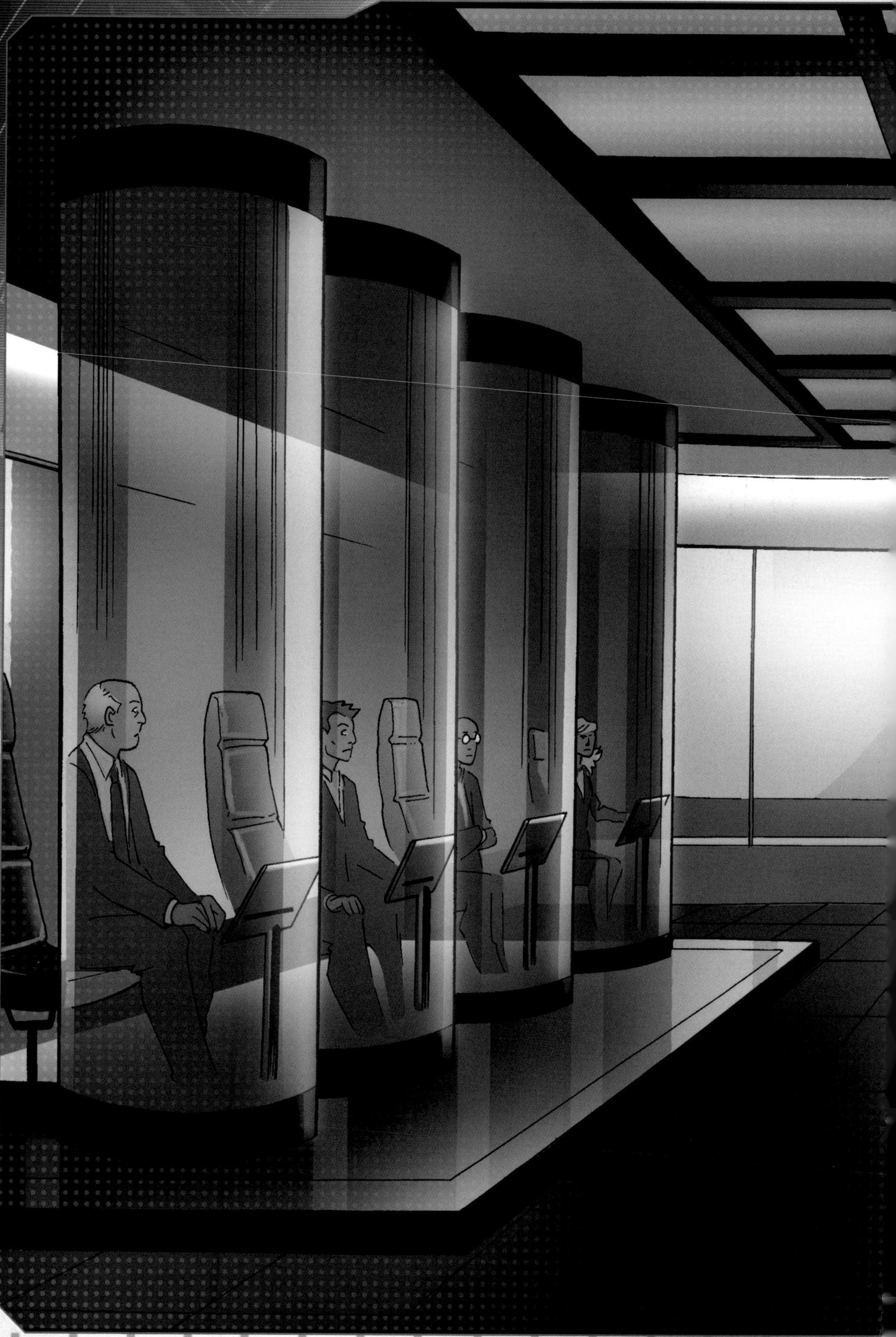

IN THE WORLD SECURITY COUNCIL CHAMBERS, Secretary Alexander Pierce held court in front of four large screens, each showing a different council member from various countries: the United States, China, India, and Britain. The council was upset that a French pirate had been able to hijack a covert S.H.I.E.L.D. vessel.

Pierce explained that he did not care about one boat, he cared about the fleet. "If this council intends to fall to rancor every time someone pushes us on the playground, then maybe we need someone to oversee us," he said.

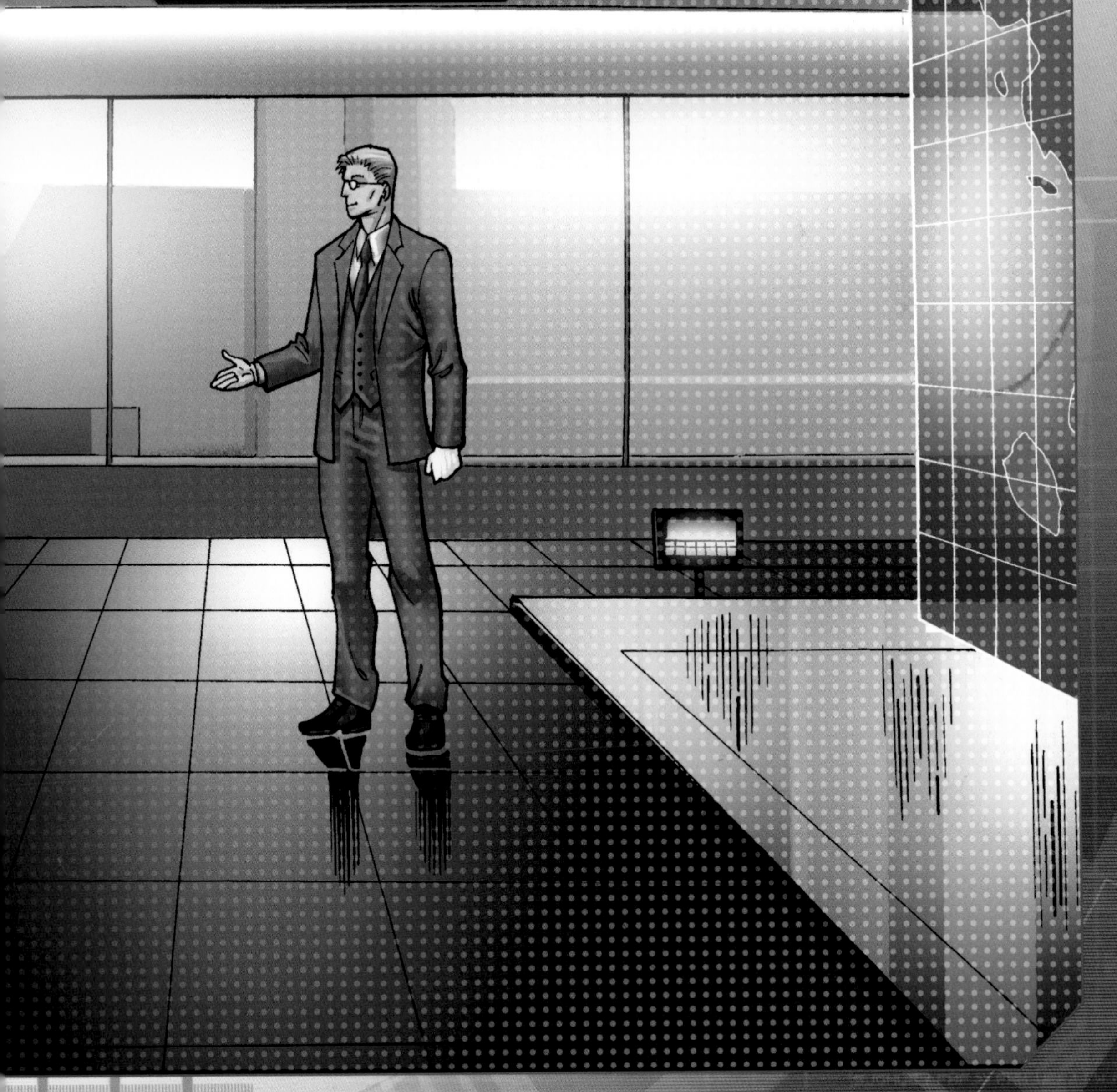

An assistant approached and whispered to Pierce that Nick Fury was waiting outside. Pierce left the council members to argue among themselves as he stepped out to greet his old friend.

Fury cut straight to the point: he needed to ask Pierce a favor. Steve's concerns had been weighing on him. Maybe this is a path S.H.I.E.L.D. shouldn't go down, Fury thought. He asked Pierce to delay the launch so that he could make sure that there would be no bugs in the system.

Pierce said the council would take a bit of convincing, but he would get the delay Fury needed.

As Nick Fury traveled home in his SUV, he grew concerned; he felt like he was being followed. He activated a hologram display—which could read license plates and run facial scans—on his windshield to ensure no enemies could get the jump on him. Fury then dialed Maria Hill, one of his most trusted agents, whose hologram suddenly appeared on his windshield. Fury asked her to keep her eyes open, because he felt something was wrong.

"Deep Shadow conditions," Nick cryptically said.

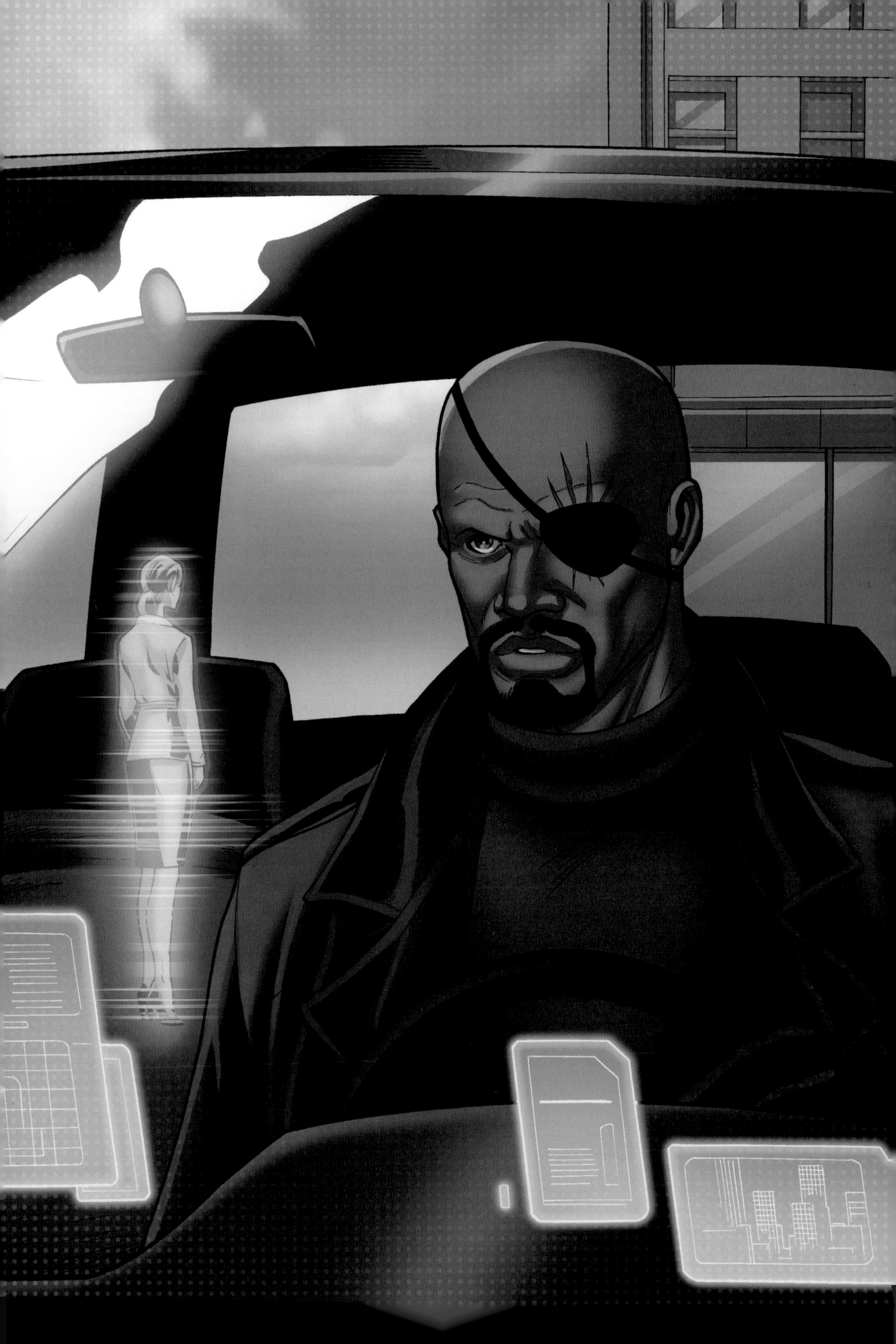

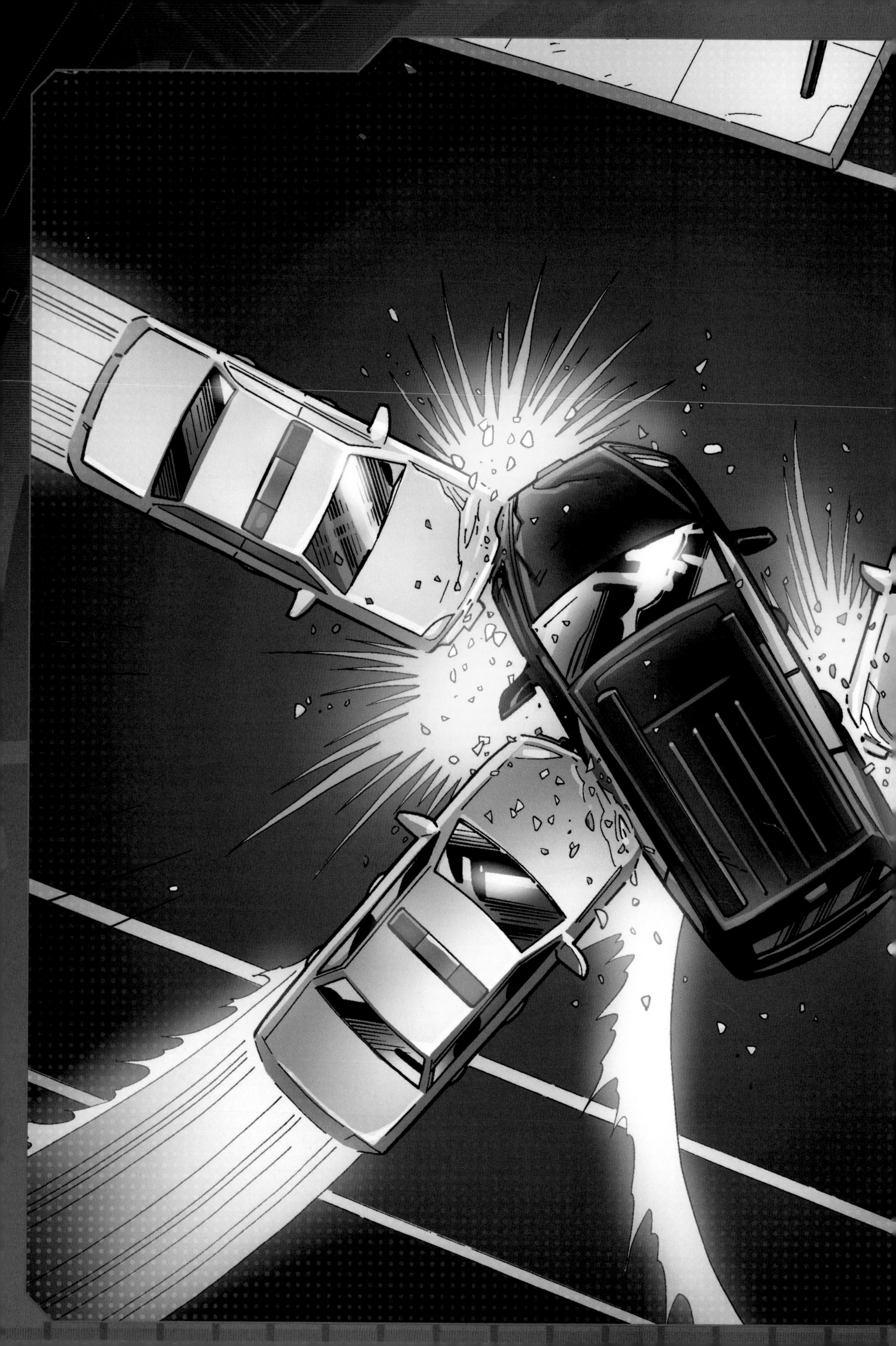

Before Maria could respond, a police car SMASHED Nick from one side—followed by another, and another! The three police cars blocked him from going anywhere. Fury, stunned, asked himself: Why would the police be attacking me?

CRASH!
KABOOOOOOM!
CRSSHHHHHHH!

9022-REQ_021-32_LM45

KTL_0-4T3O-P9-L2_GFL2

00_T8-2044T9_00-KJS-0

NICK FURY THEN SAW MEN IN MERCENARY OUTFITS get out of the squad cars. These are definitely not police officers, Fury thought. Two mercenaries attached a menacing device to the ground next to the SUV. It was a battering ram, which began smashing in the driver's side door so that the mercs could get to Fury!

BAM! BAM! BAM!

The car slowly started to crush in on him! Nick was trapped with no way out! His SUV was stuck, he was surrounded by dangerous mercenaries, and they were about to break in and grab him! Thinking quickly, Fury activated the SUV's countermeasures, and the car instantly jolted to life, propelling forward and smashing through the police cars!

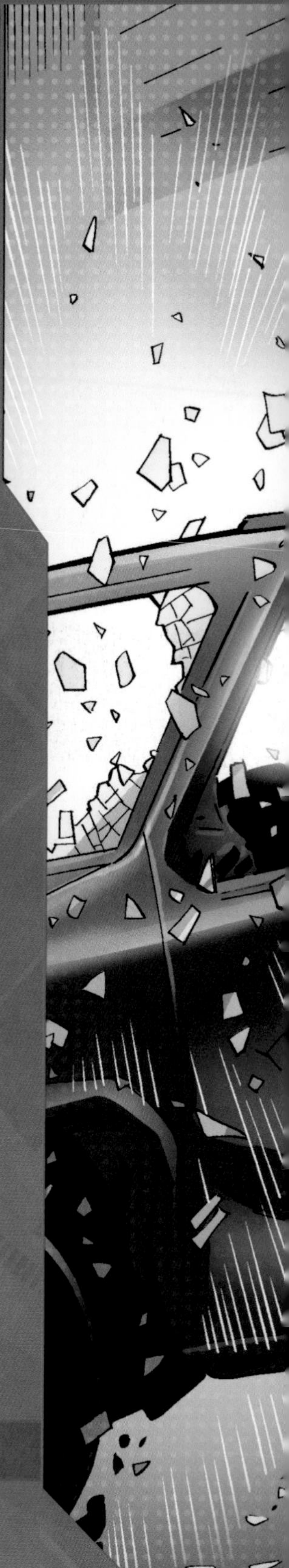

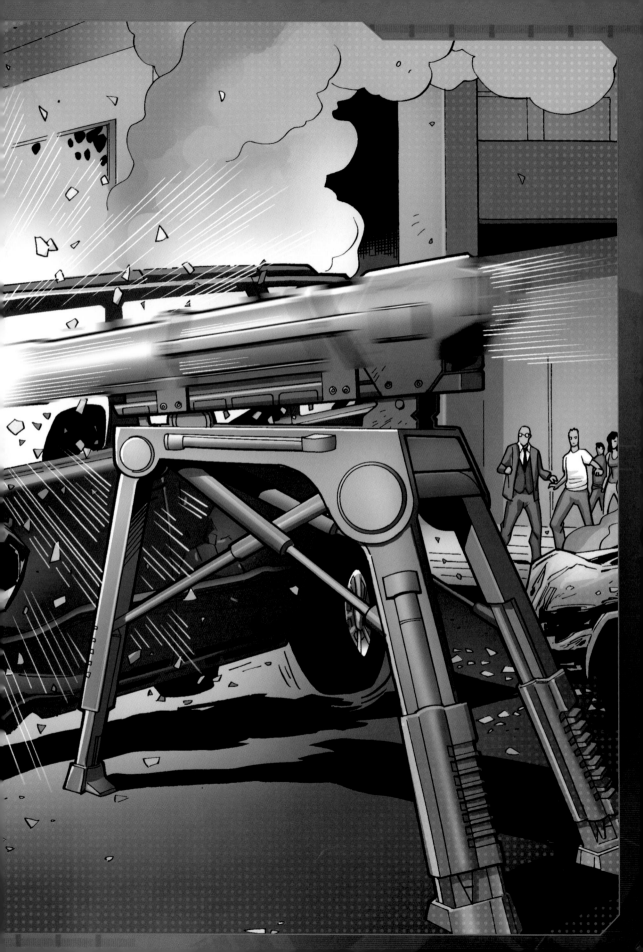

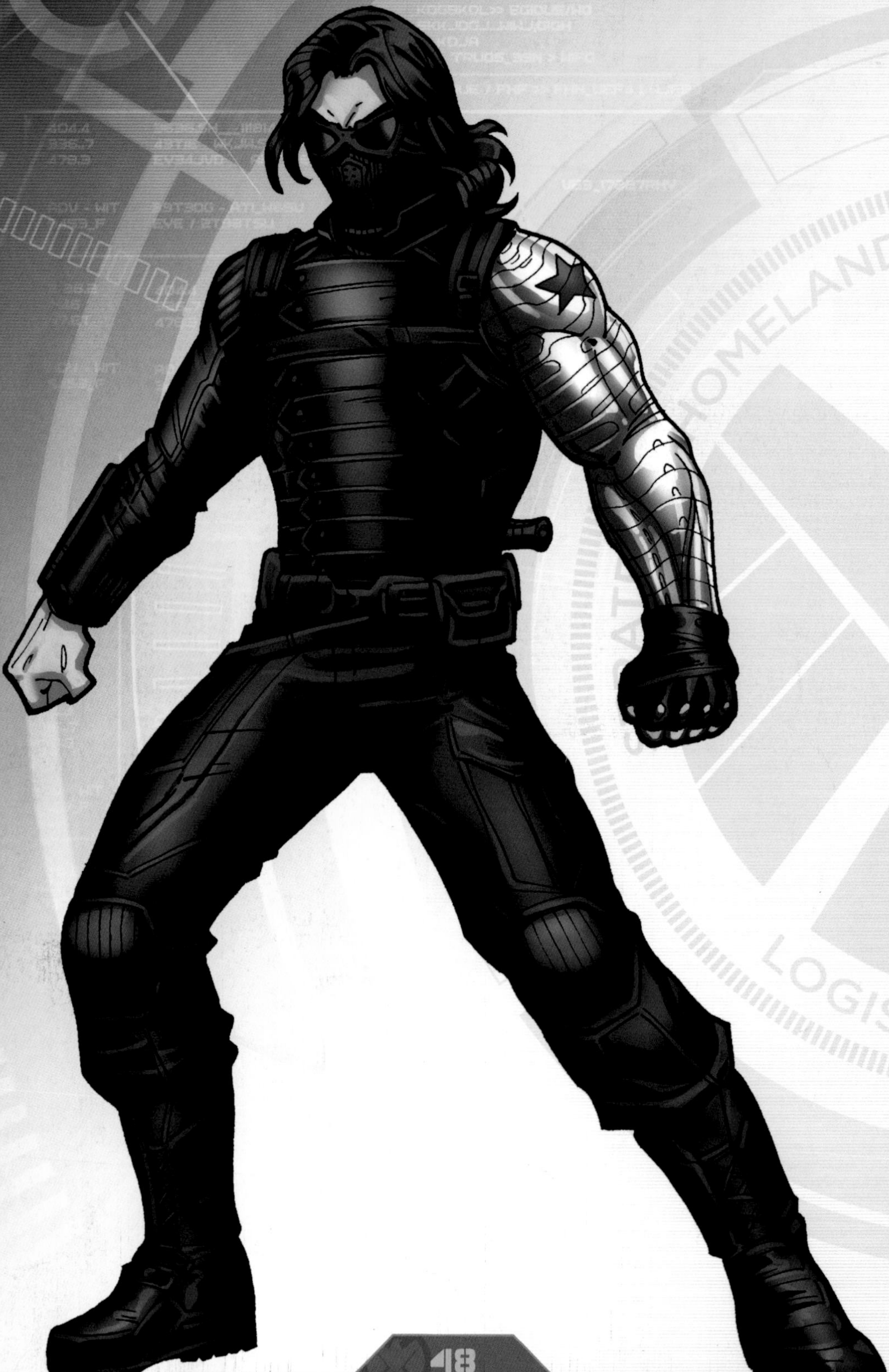

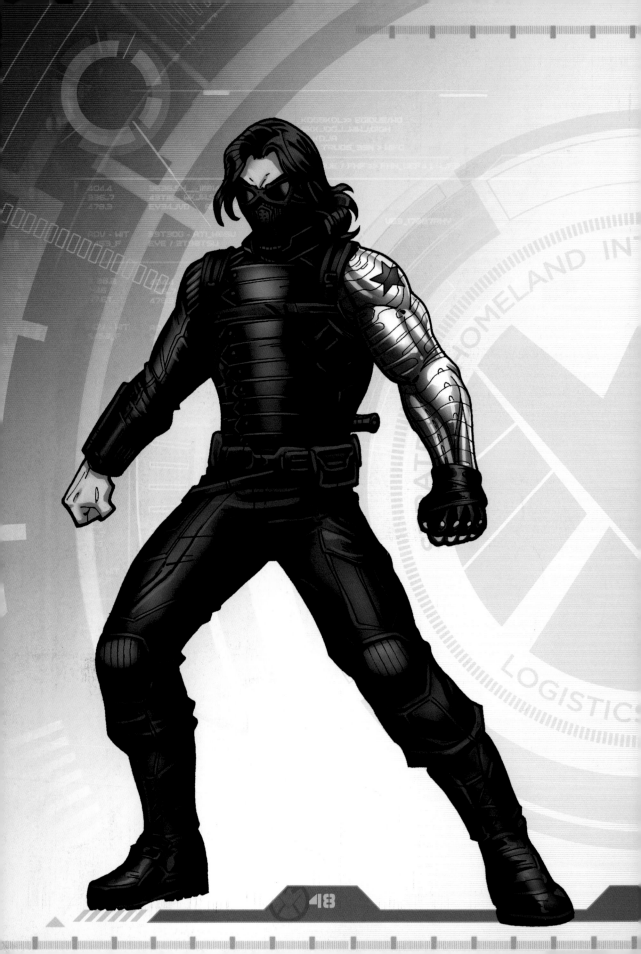

Fury drove away from the mercenaries as quickly as he could, but his windshield display alerted him to an enemy on the road just ahead. It was a **MASKED MAN** who had just pulled out a high-tech rocket launcher! The figure fired a black disc from the launcher. It skidded down the street and landed under Fury's SUV.

This can't be good, Fury thought as the disc **EXPLODED,** causing the SUV to cartwheel and slide to a stop on its hood!

Nick Fury tried to get his bearings as he saw a pair of black boots approach. He yelled a command to the SUV's computer as a shining metal arm wrenched the driver's door off the car.

The masked man prepared to snatch Fury out of the SUV but noticed he was **GONE!** Inside, a perfect circle glowed green where Fury had sliced a hole in the roof . . . and the street below.

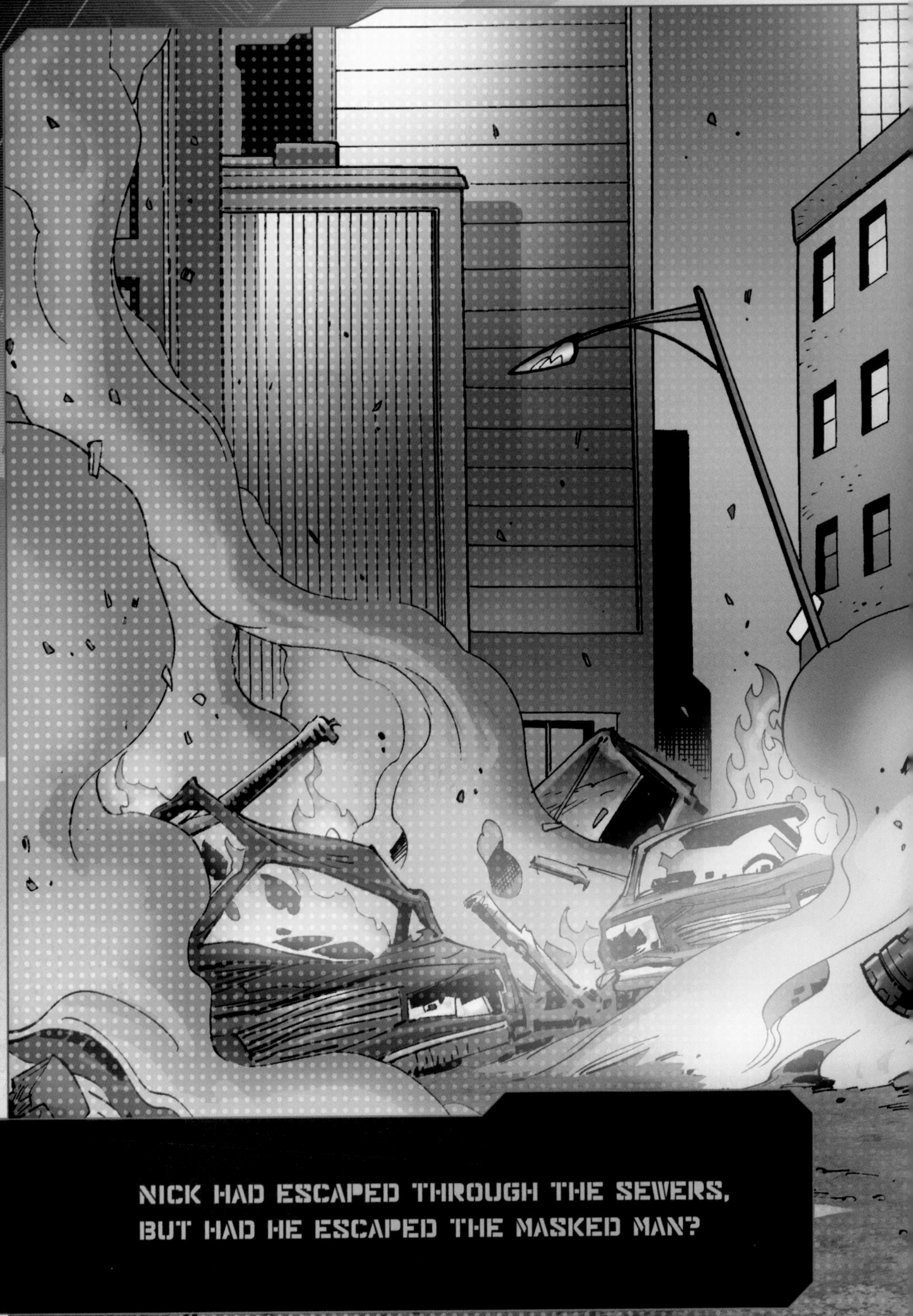
NICK HAD ESCAPED THROUGH THE SEWERS,
BUT HAD HE ESCAPED THE MASKED MAN?

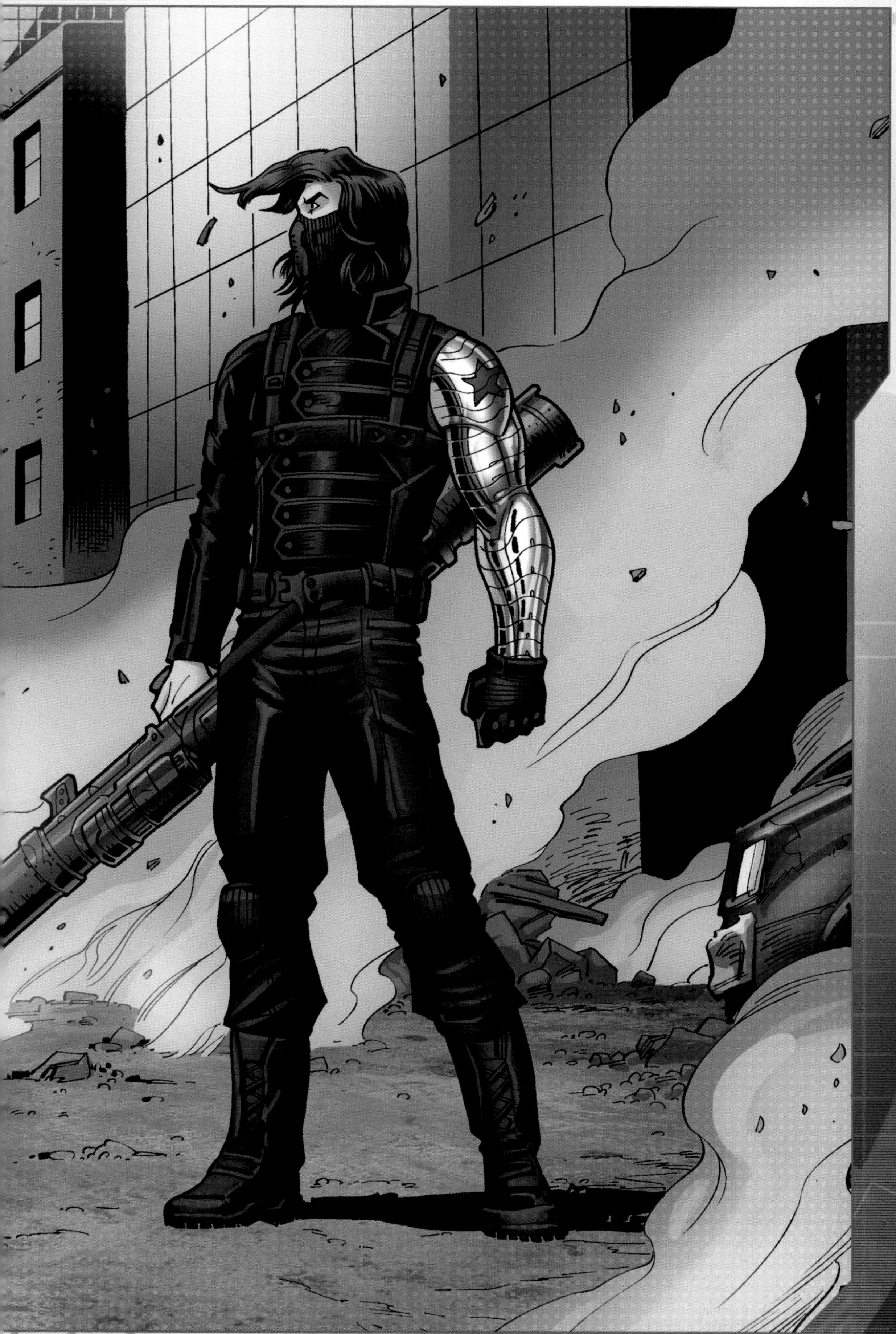

LATER THAT NIGHT, Steve Rogers pulled up to his apartment on his motorcycle. As he walked to his door, he noticed music coming from inside. That's strange, Steve thought. Concerned, he entered through a fire escape.

His shield at the ready, Steve crept into his dark living room and was surprised to find Nick Fury, battered and bruised, on his couch. Fury was concerned someone might be listening, thus the music. But to be even safer, he began to speak in code.

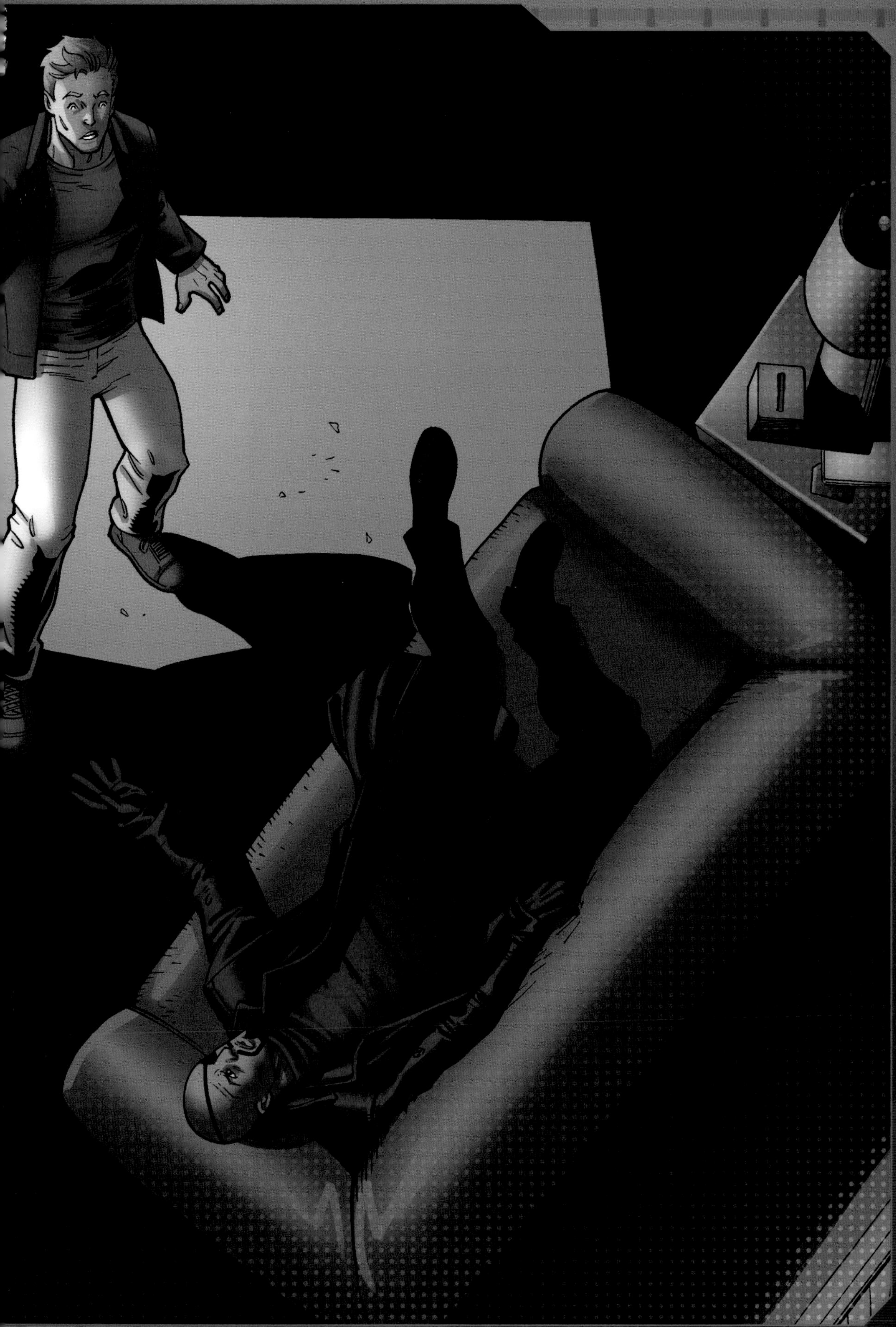

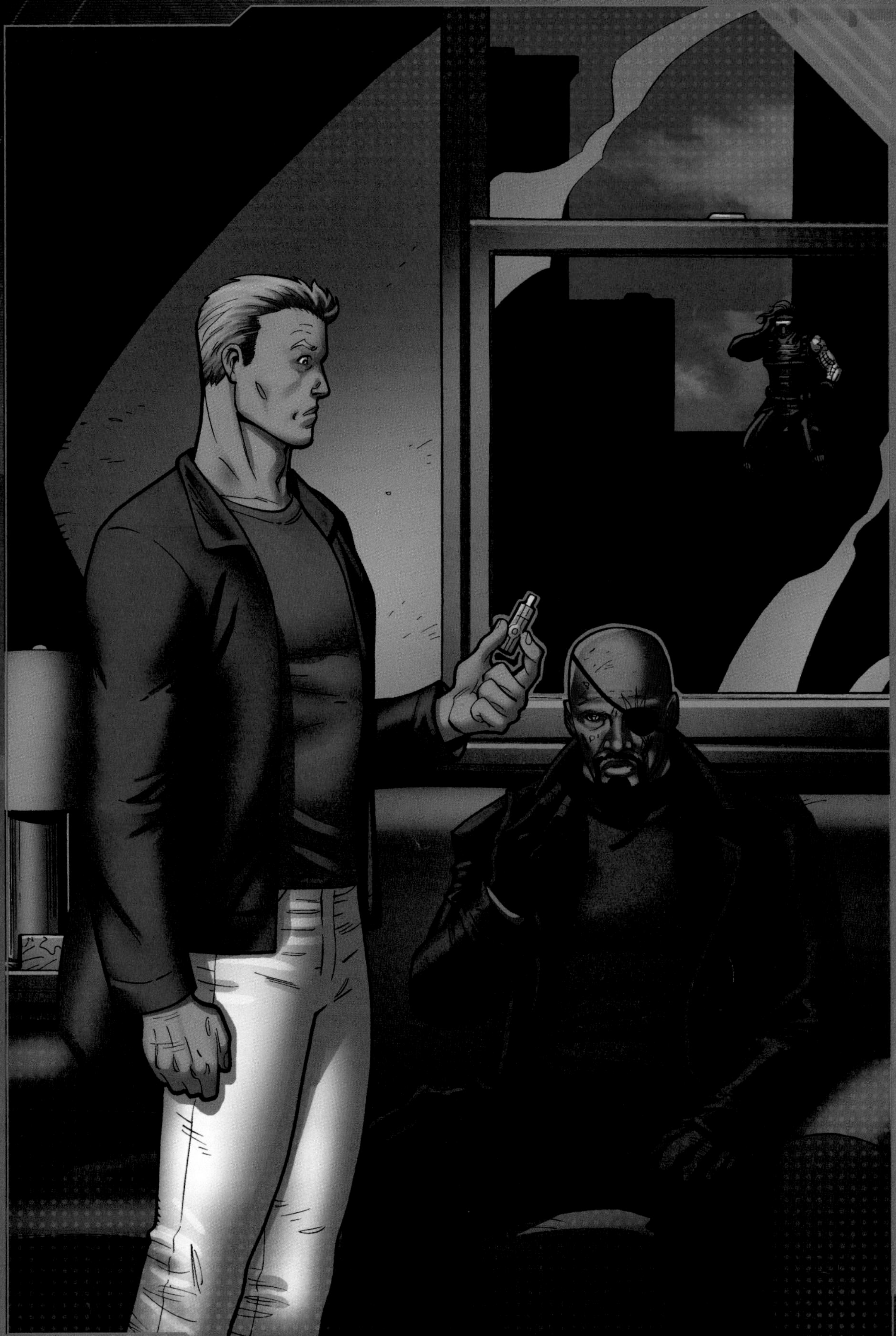

IMG003_TF

As Fury carried on a casual, friendly conversation with a baffled Steve, he typed a different conversation into his phone. Fury held up the S.H.I.E.L.D. data drive and through his phone told Steve that a masked man was after it.

Nick explained that there was top secret S.H.I.E.L.D. information on the data drive. He needed Steve to protect it and get it to a safe place while they figured out who was after it. His injuries finally getting the better of him, Nick passed out.

Just then, Steve noticed the MASKED MAN watching from an adjacent rooftop. That's him! Steve burst through the window and went up the fire escape to the roof where he HURLED his shield at him!

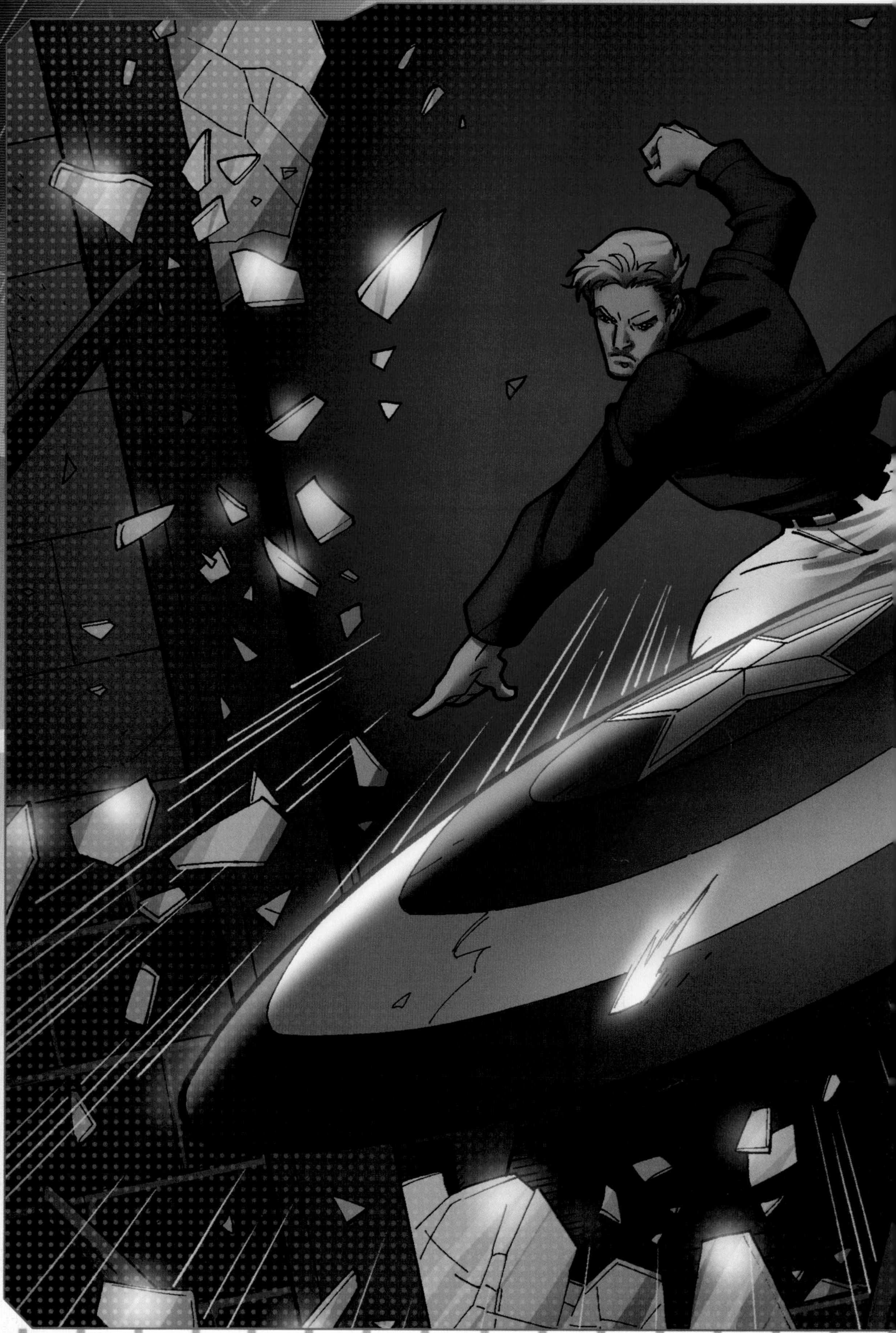

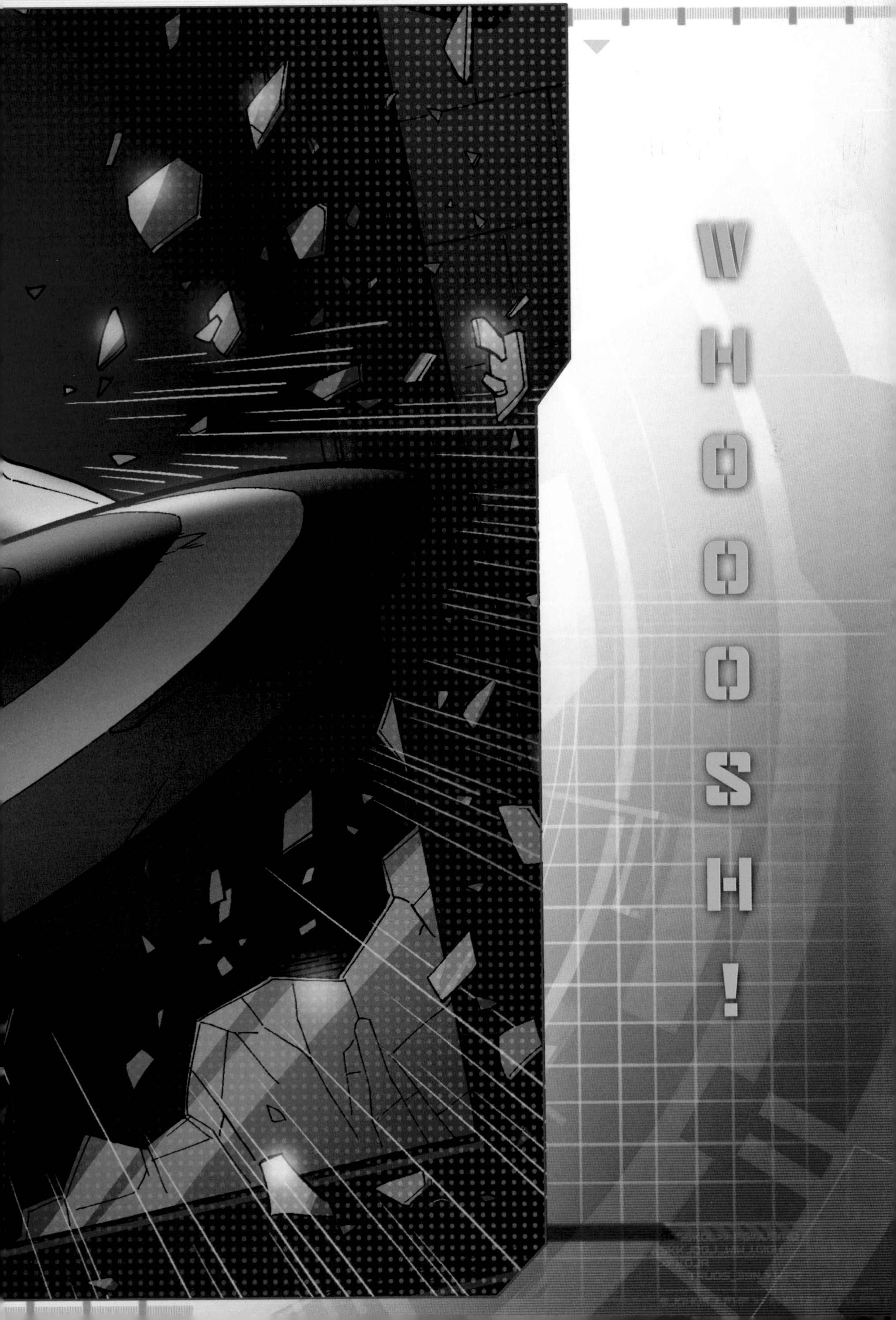
WHOOOSH!

The masked man plucked it right out of the air with a **CLANG!** His arm was made entirely of metal!

Steve stared, shocked. No one had ever been able to catch his shield. The masked man stared back and then **WHIPPED** the shield at Steve, who caught it, sending him skidding back across the roof. Steve looked up to find that the mystery man was gone. Whoever he was, Steve knew he would see him again.

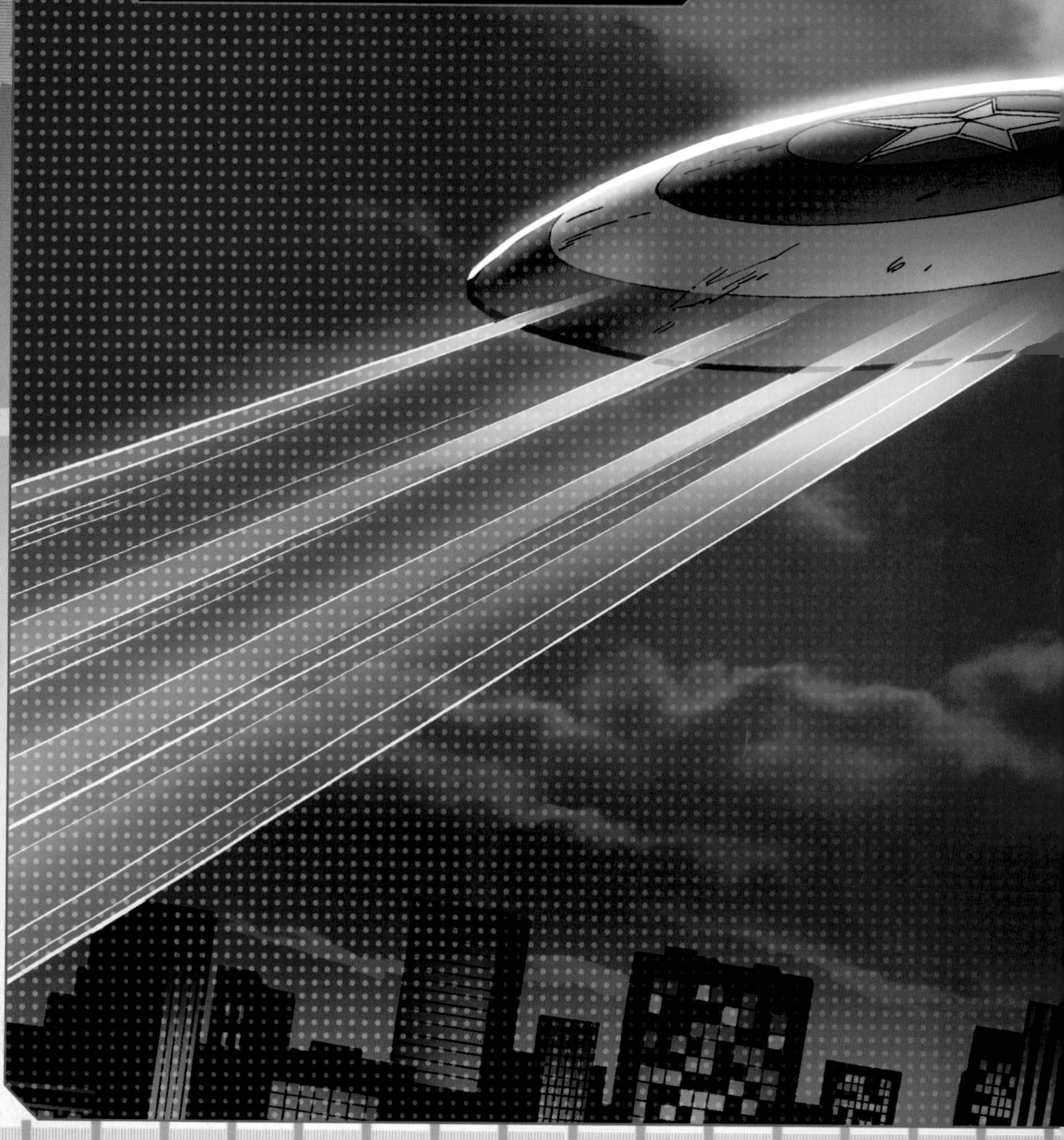

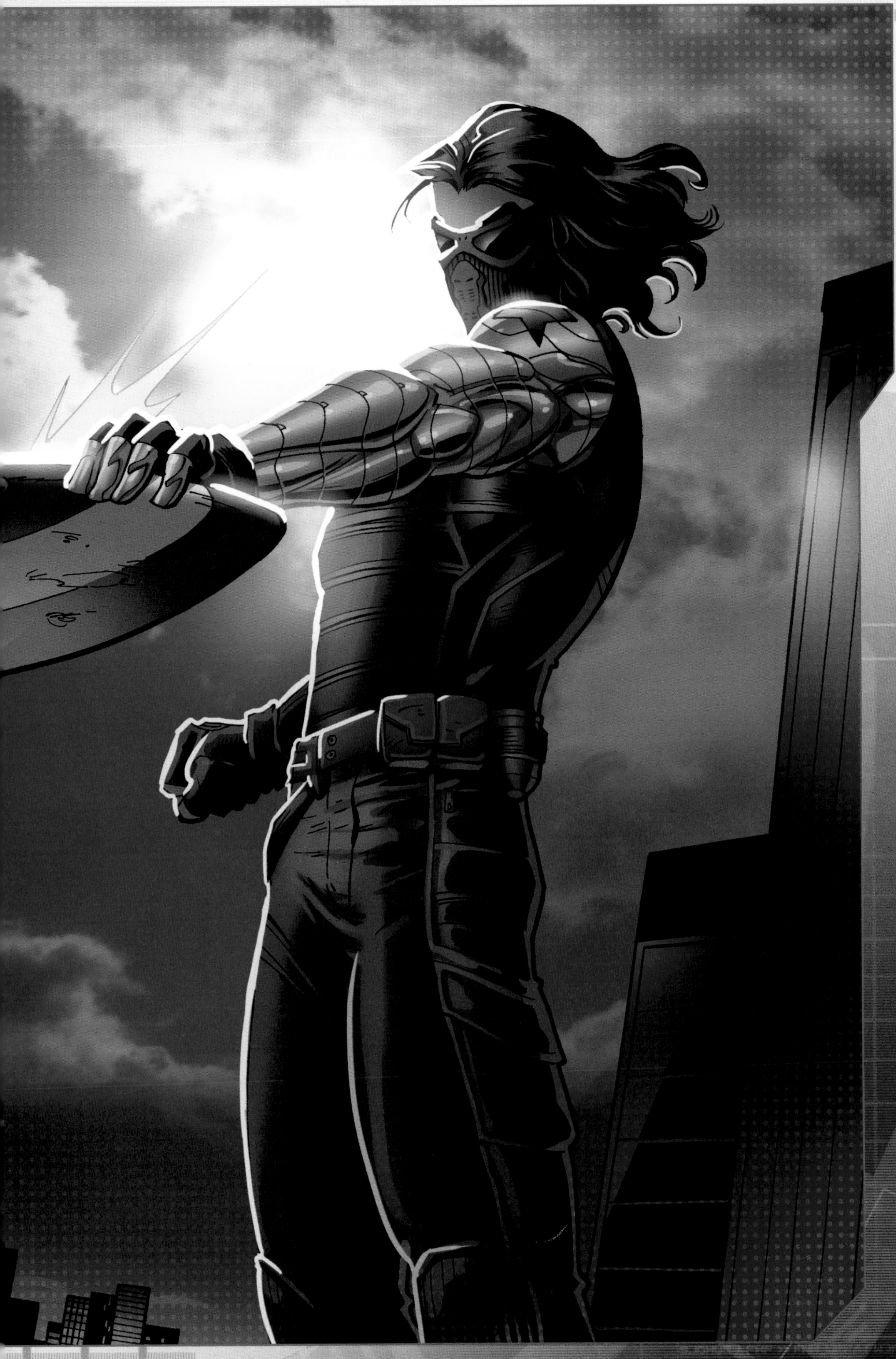

CONCERNED, Natasha Romanoff ran into the hospital where Nick Fury had been taken. Steve was already there in the waiting room. Natasha asked Steve where Fury was. Steve explained that Fury had some severe injuries, and he was currently in surgery. The doctors didn't know if he would make it.

Natasha asked him what had happened, and Steve told her about the masked man with the metal arm. When Steve said that, Natasha remembered being attacked by the same man five years earlier in the Middle East.

"Most of the intelligence community doesn't believe he exists," she explained. "The ones who do call him the Winter Soldier."

"So he's a ghost story?" Steve asked.

"Going after him is a dead end. I've tried. Like you said, he's a ghost," Natasha replied.

Steve showed the data drive in his hand to Natasha. This was what the ghost was after. He needed her help finding a safe place to stash it while they looked for the Winter Soldier. Steve knew he had to get revenge for what the masked man had done to the Director of S.H.I.E.L.D.

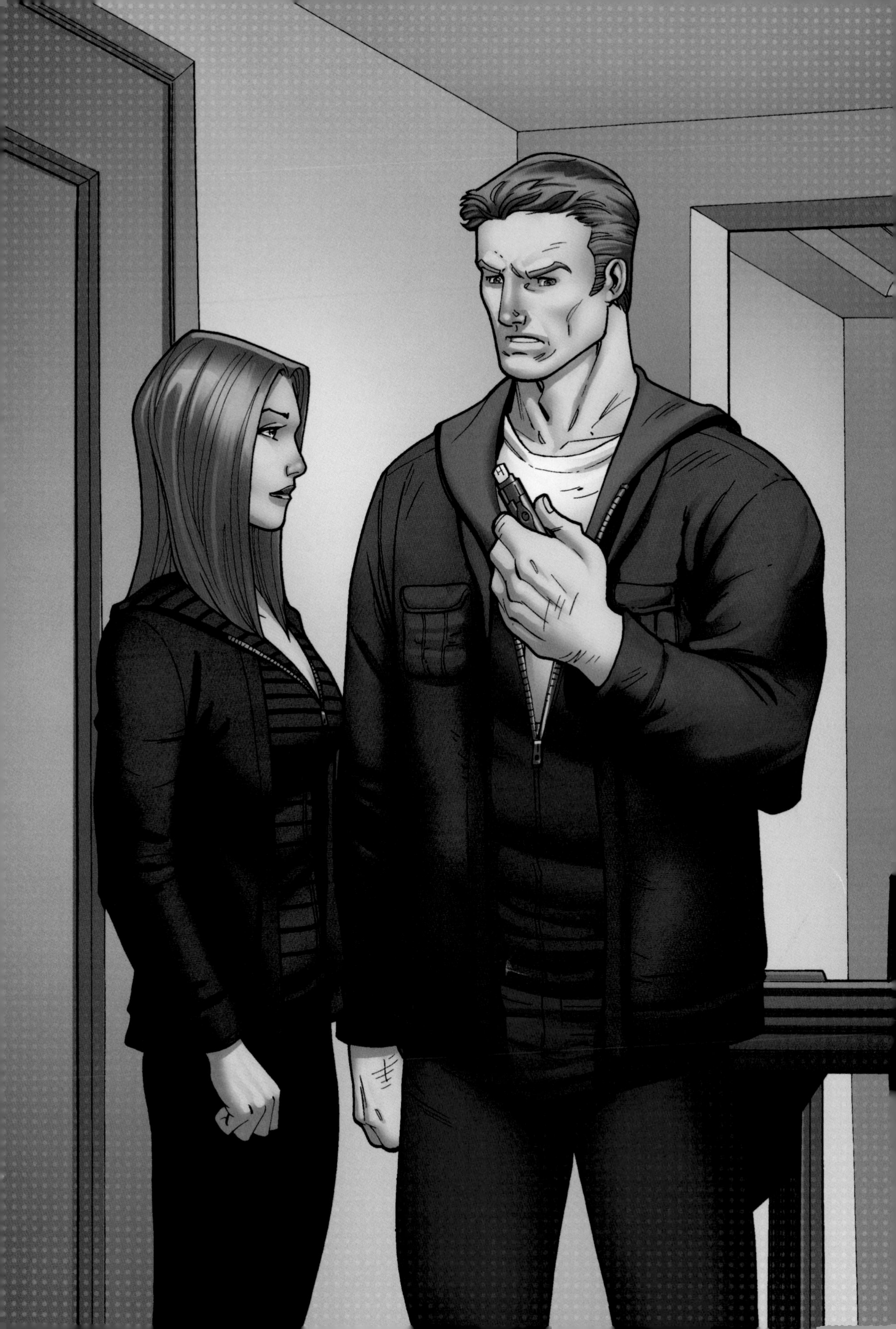

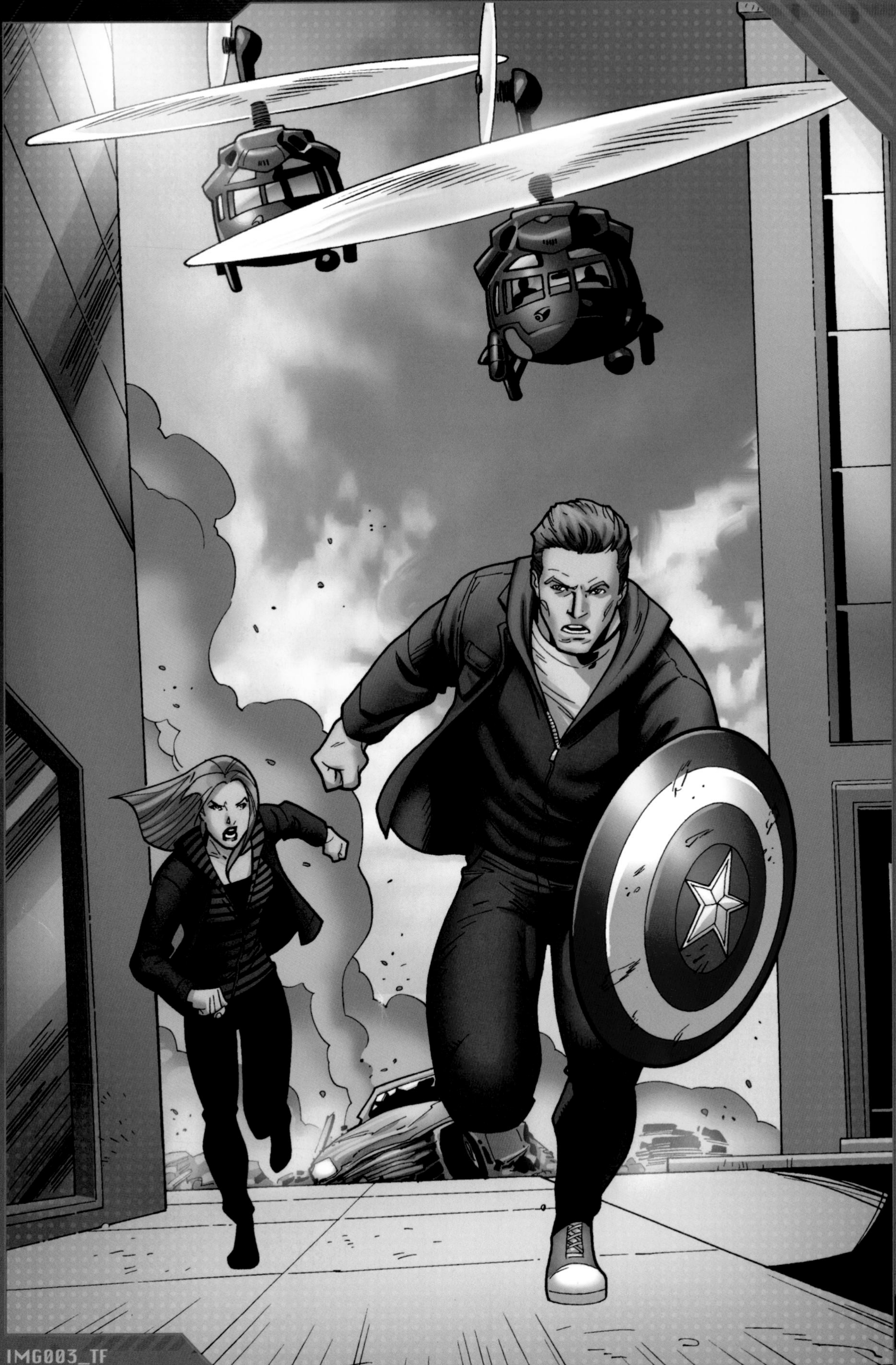

IMG003_TF

Steve and Natasha drove down the freeway, discussing where they could hide the data drive. Suddenly, two high-tech helicopters roared overhead. It was the Winter Soldier and his mercenaries!

Natasha took evasive action, trying to lose the helicopters. She sped past cars and trucks as Steve readied his shield. He **HURLED** it at the lead helicopter. It broke the glass windshield before it ricocheted and returned to him. The second helicopter advanced, with the Winter Soldier shouting orders. Steve looked up and saw a merc aiming a high-powered grenade launcher right at them! Knowing that the car was about to be hit by a missile, Steve grabbed Natasha and they jumped out of the speeding vehicle.

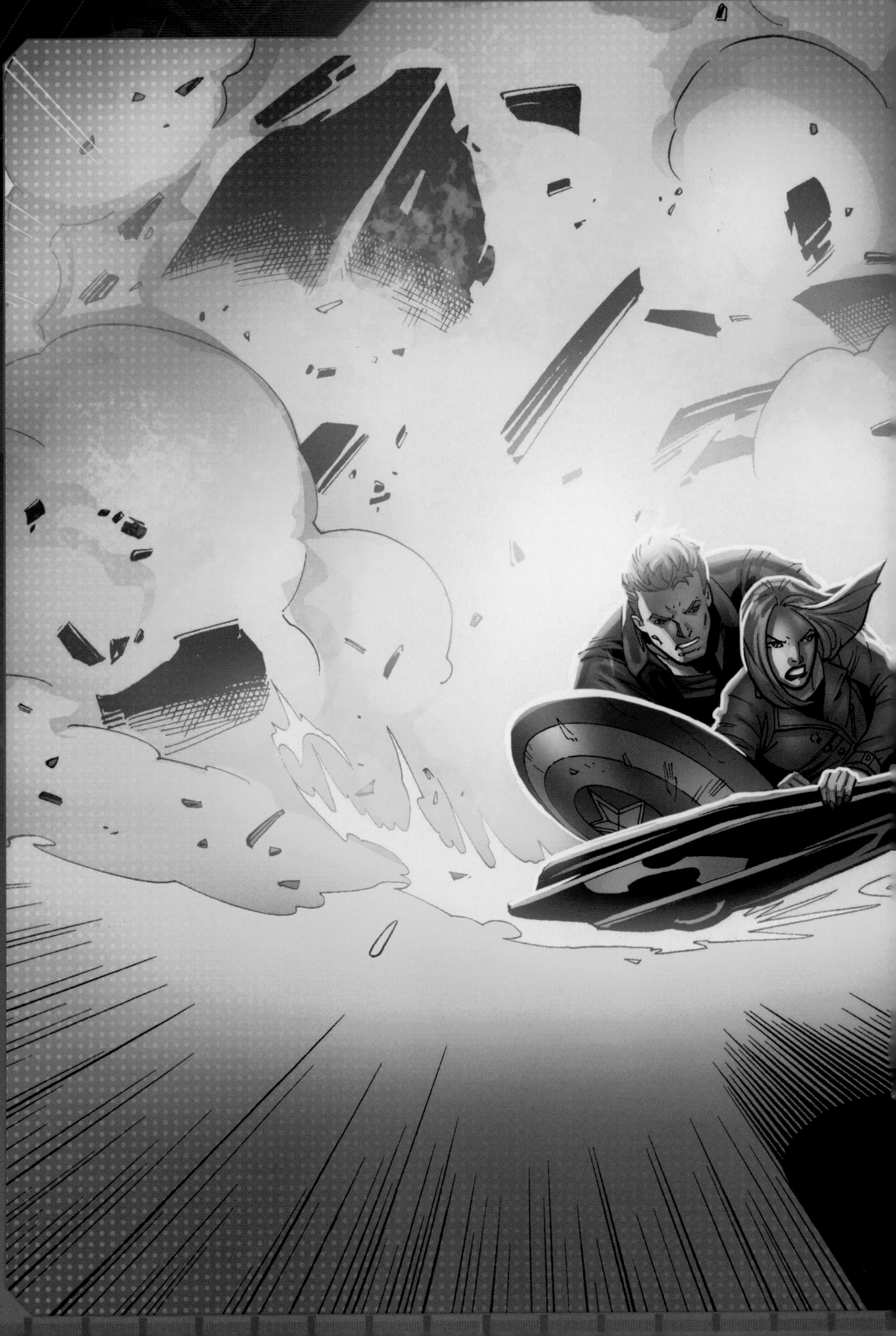

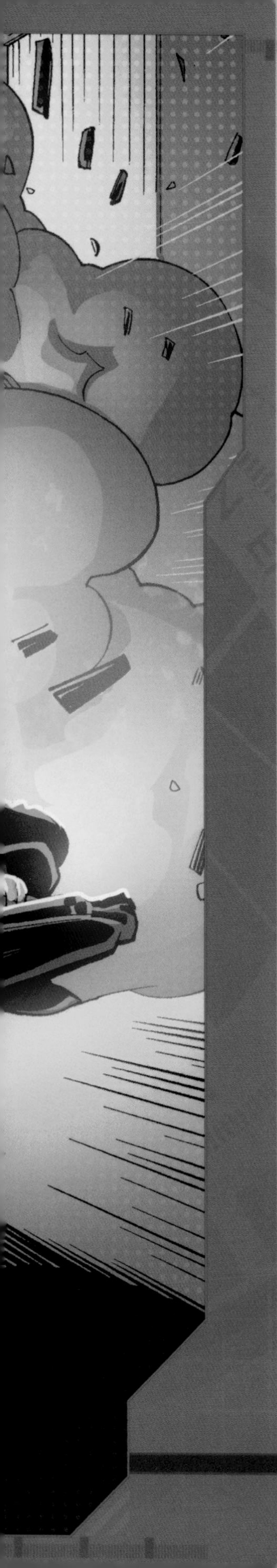

The merc fired the grenade launcher and a missile collided into the side of their sports car!

A huge explosion destroyed the car as Steve and Natasha slid to a safe stop aboard his shield.

Using the flames as a distraction, Steve and Natasha quickly escaped into the nearby woods as the helicopters landed. The Winter Soldier and his mercenaries hopped out and looked through the rubble, trying to find them. But they came up empty-handed. The S.H.I.E.L.D. agents had escaped with the data drive.

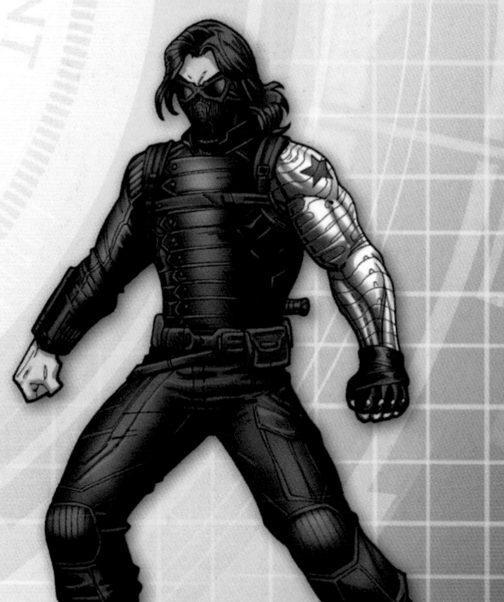

THE NEXT MORNING, faces dirty and clothes torn, Steve and Natasha arrived at Sam Wilson's door. Steve remembered that if he ever needed someone to talk to, he could turn to Sam. They needed a place to lie low, and Sam was more than happy to help.

Sam cooked them breakfast as the two agents wondered what to do with the data drive. Sam offered his house as a safe place for them to hide it, but Steve was hesitant. It could be dangerous to have it there. The Winter Soldier was after it, and it held top secret S.H.I.E.L.D. files. Sam told them he was sure they could leave it there. Anything to help out a friend.

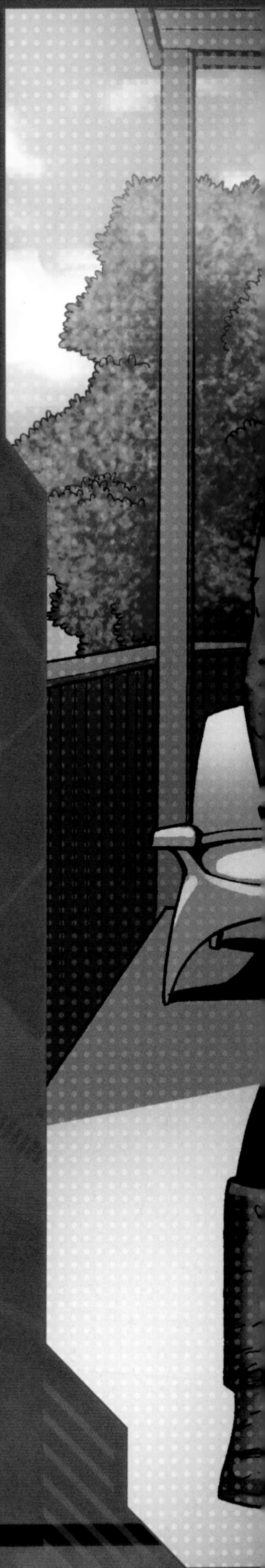

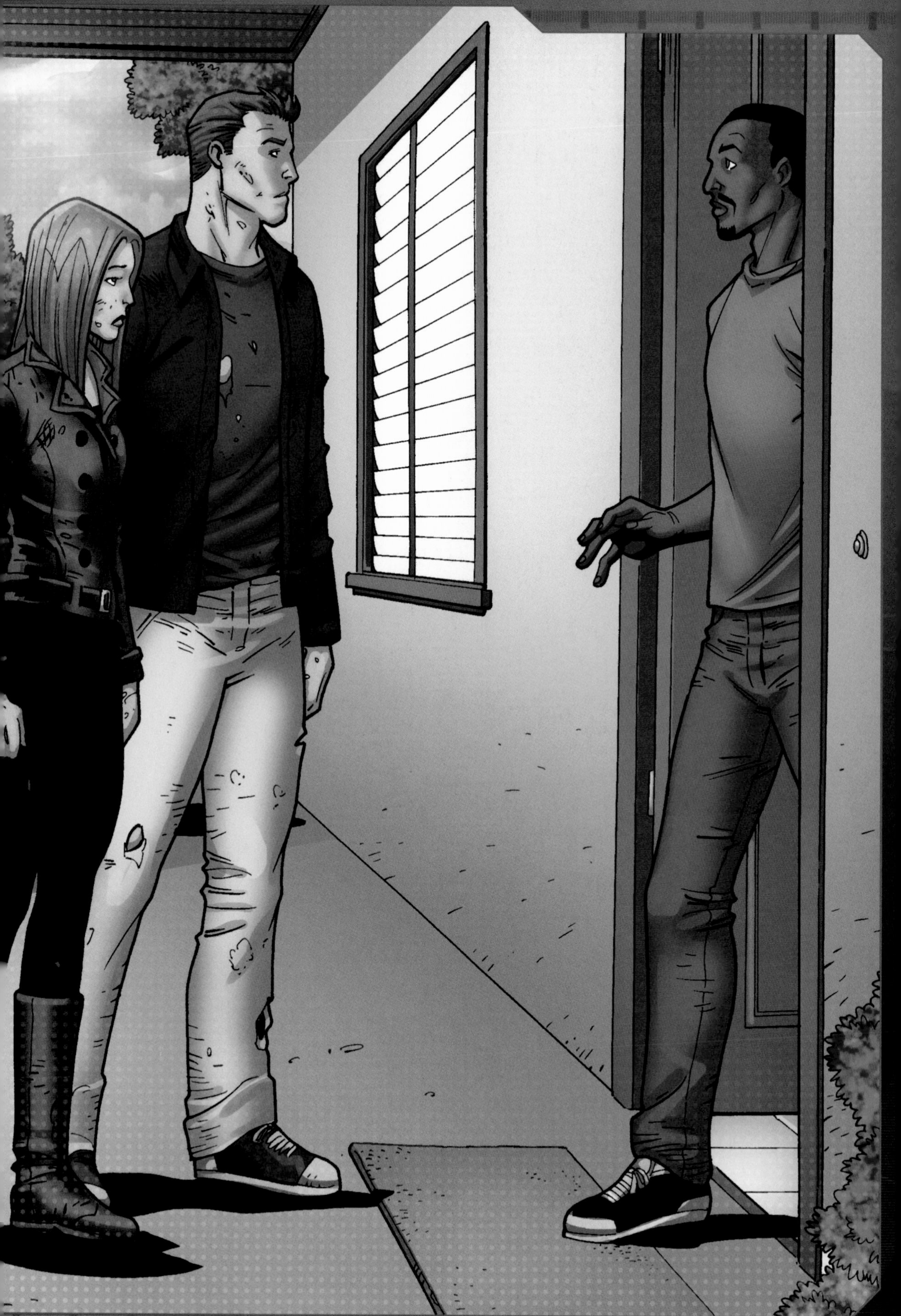

As Sam hid the data drive, Steve and Natasha discussed how to fight the Winter Soldier. He was as strong, as fast, and as tough as Steve, and in addition, he commanded a small army of mercenaries. They were clearly outmatched. Sam, overhearing this, returned to the kitchen with a file.

"What's this?" Steve asked.

"Call it a résumé," Sam replied. The file showed Sam's military pararescue experience, including a stamp reading **EXO-7 FALCON**. Steve was impressed but said that Sam had helped them enough. Steve couldn't ask Sam to put himself in further danger.

"Captain America needs my help," Sam said. "No better reason to get back out there."

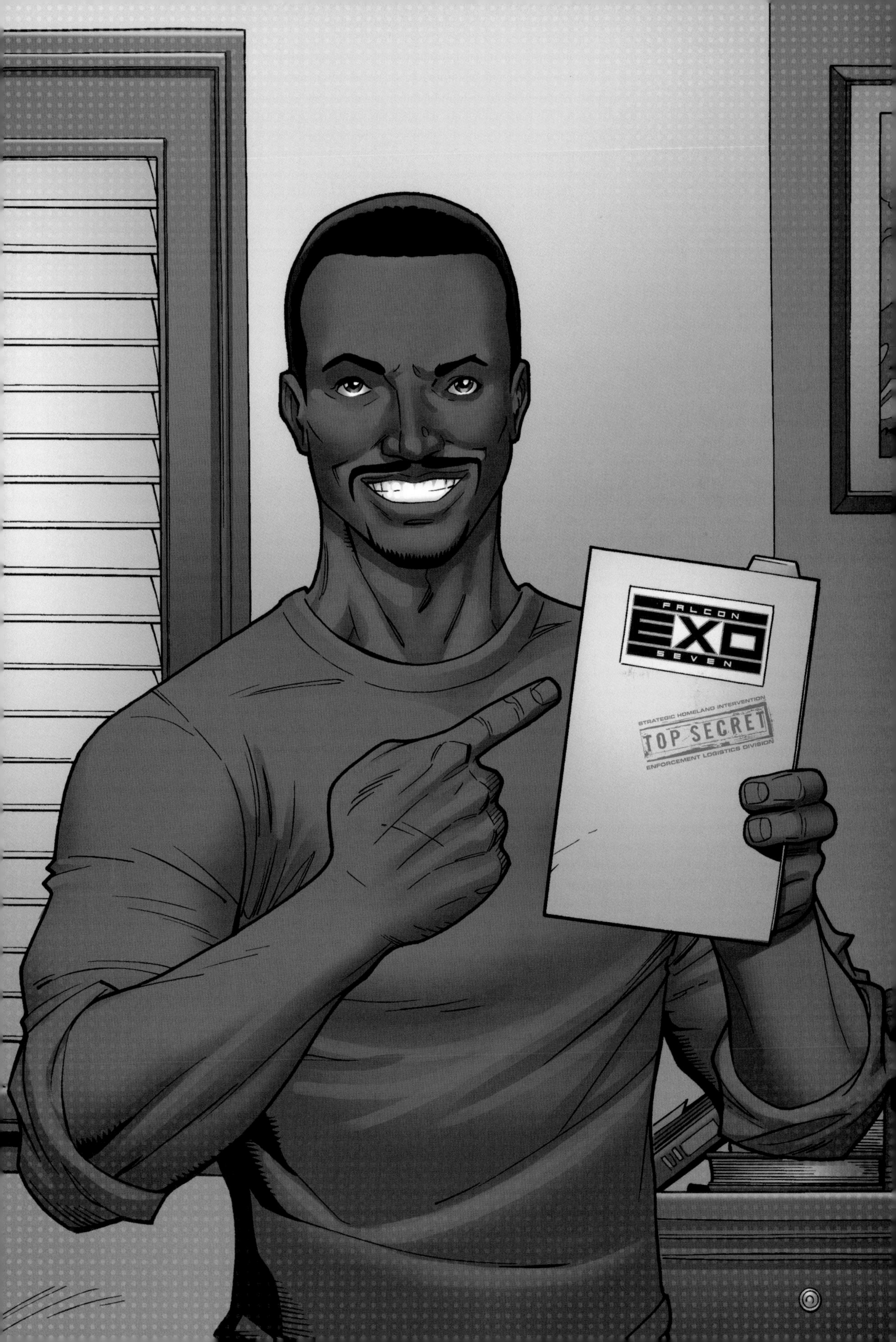
FALCON
EXO
SEVEN
STRATEGIC HOMELAND INTERVENTION
TOP SECRET
ENFORCEMENT LOGISTICS DIVISION

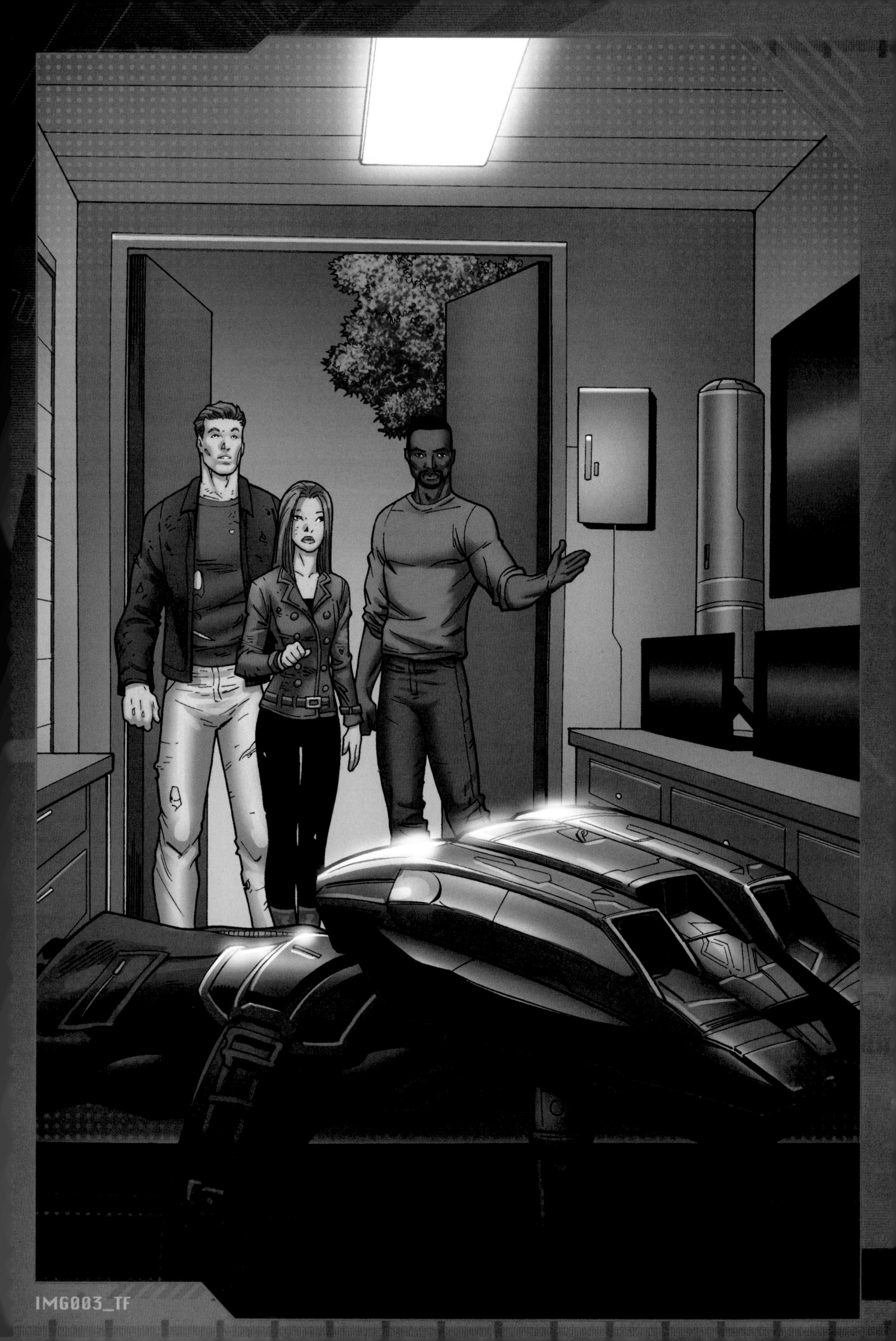
IMG003_TF

STEVE AND NATASHA FOLLOWED SAM to an old shed in his backyard. They were shocked to see Sam still had his EXO-7 FALCON suit. It was an impressive rig with a flight backpack where the polymer wings popped out.

The agents looked at each other. It would be great to have an eye in the sky, especially with the high-tech helicopters the Winter Soldier had.

"It's time. Gear up," Steve told them. "You want to fight a war, you've got to wear a uniform."

After they grabbed their suits, Captain America, Black Widow, and their new recruit went on the hunt for the Winter Soldier.

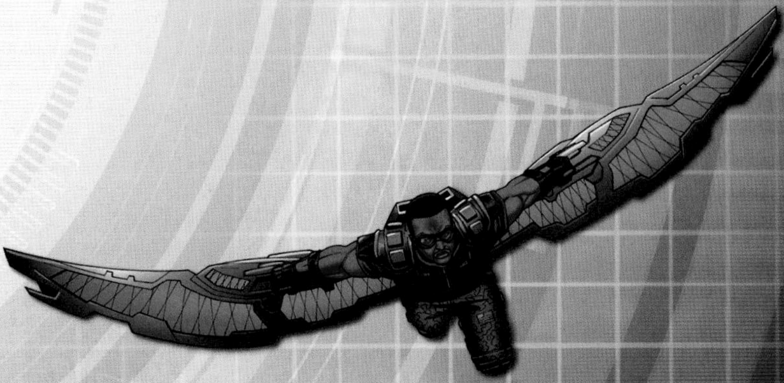

Sam flew through the sky in his Falcon suit, rising over the buildings of downtown Washington, D.C. He was keeping an eye out for any trace of Winter Soldier and his mercenaries as Cap and Black Widow ran across the rooftops. But Falcon, as he was now called, didn't have to look for long before one of the masked man's high-tech helicopters soared down to greet them with dangerous intent.

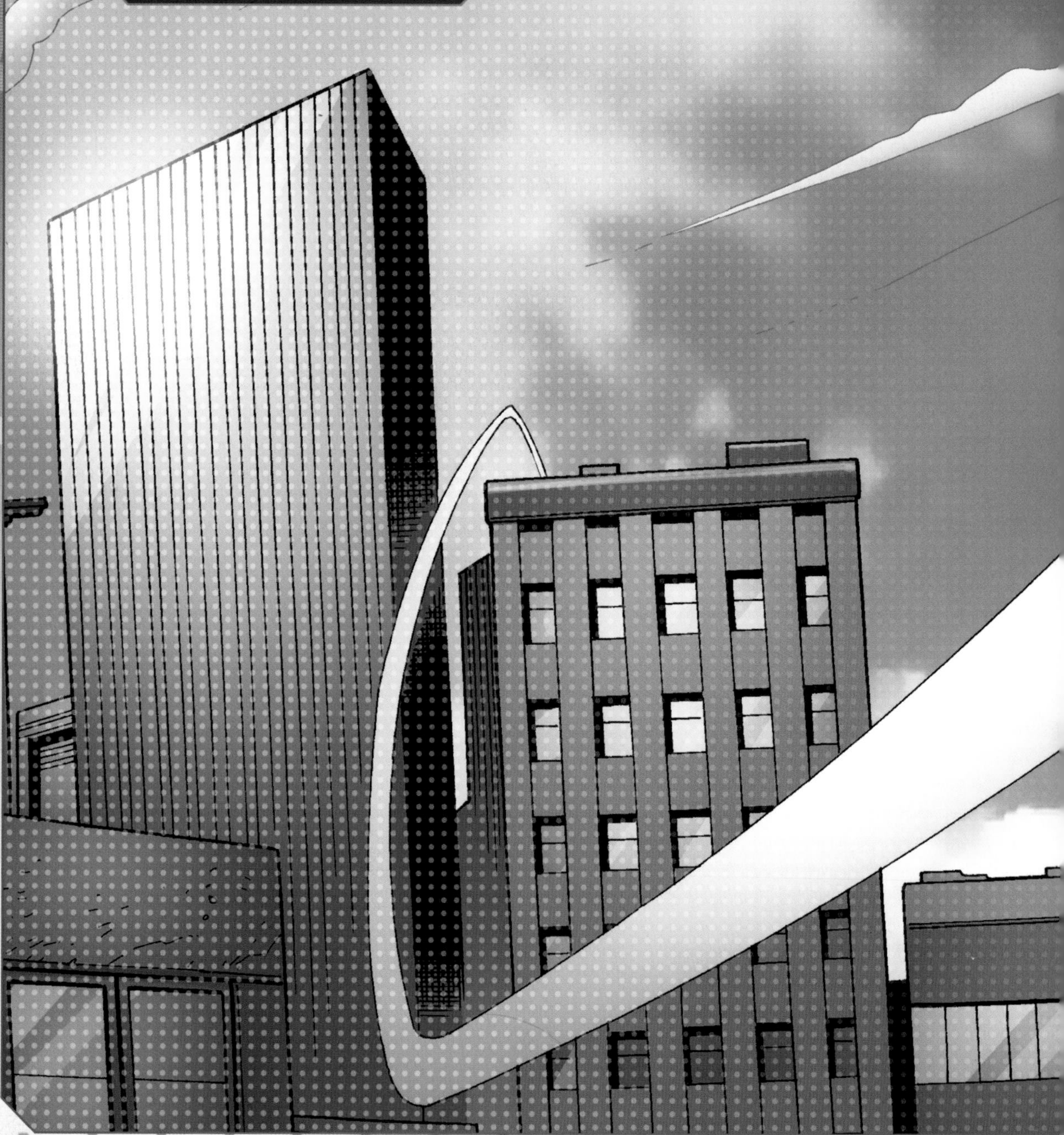

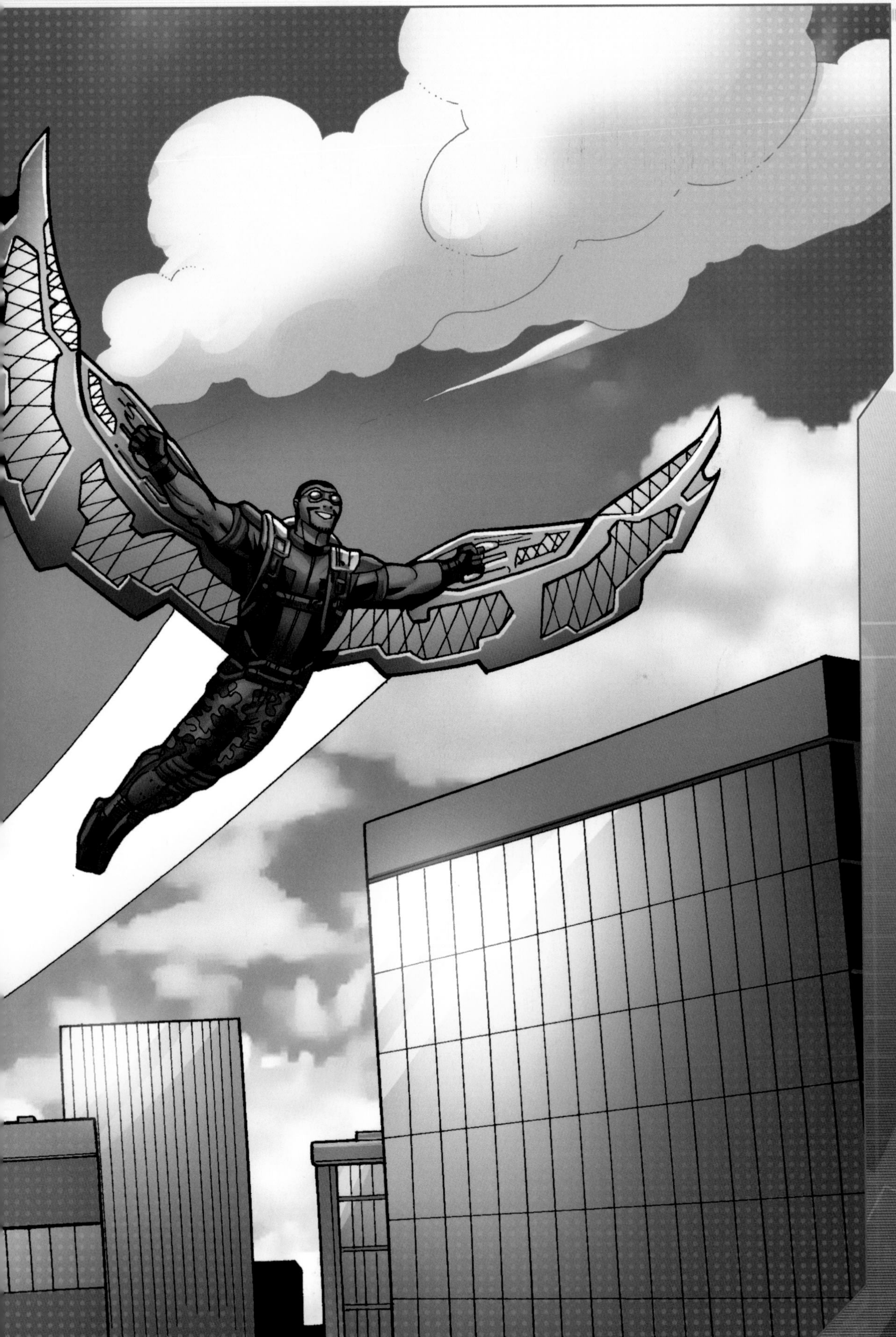

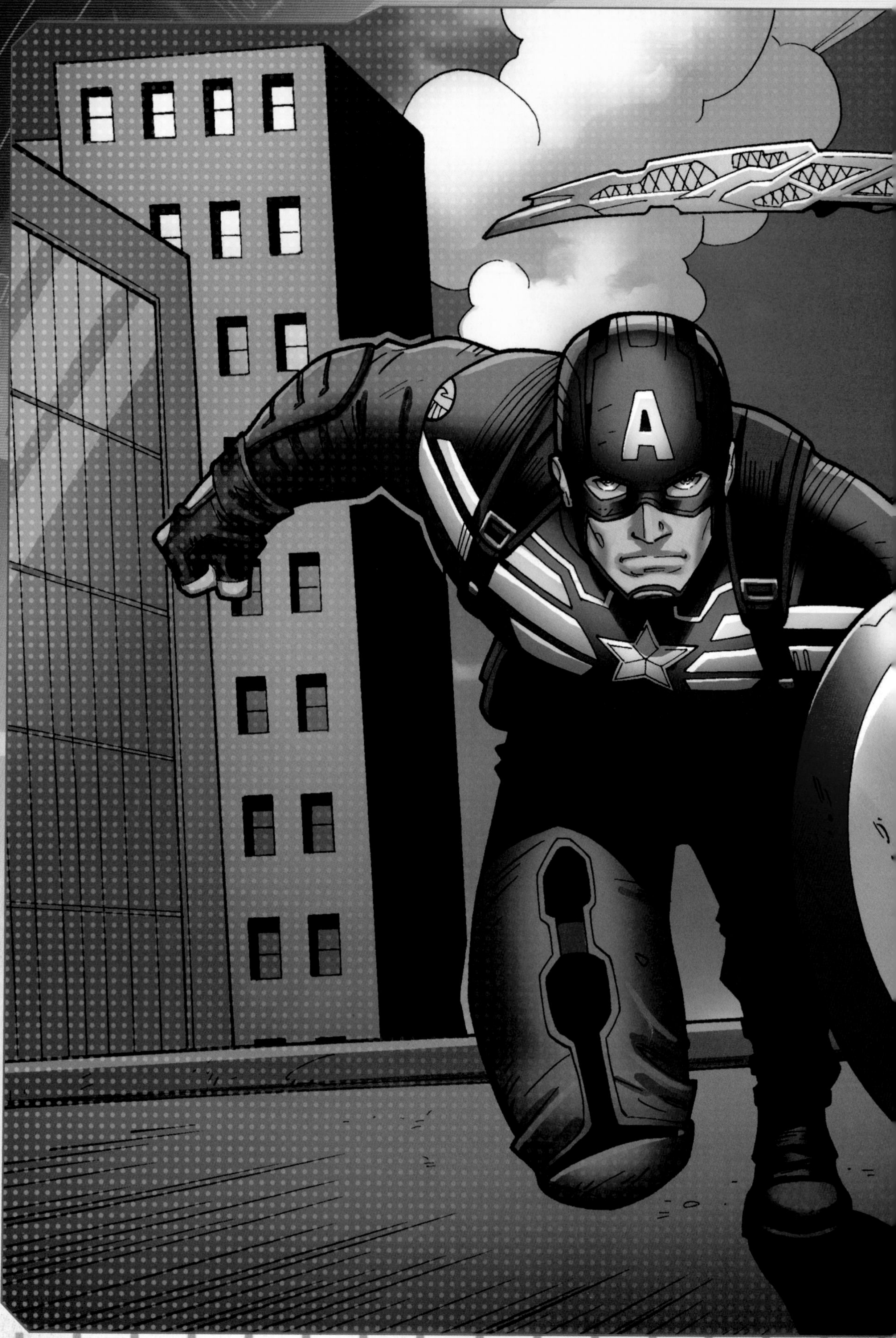

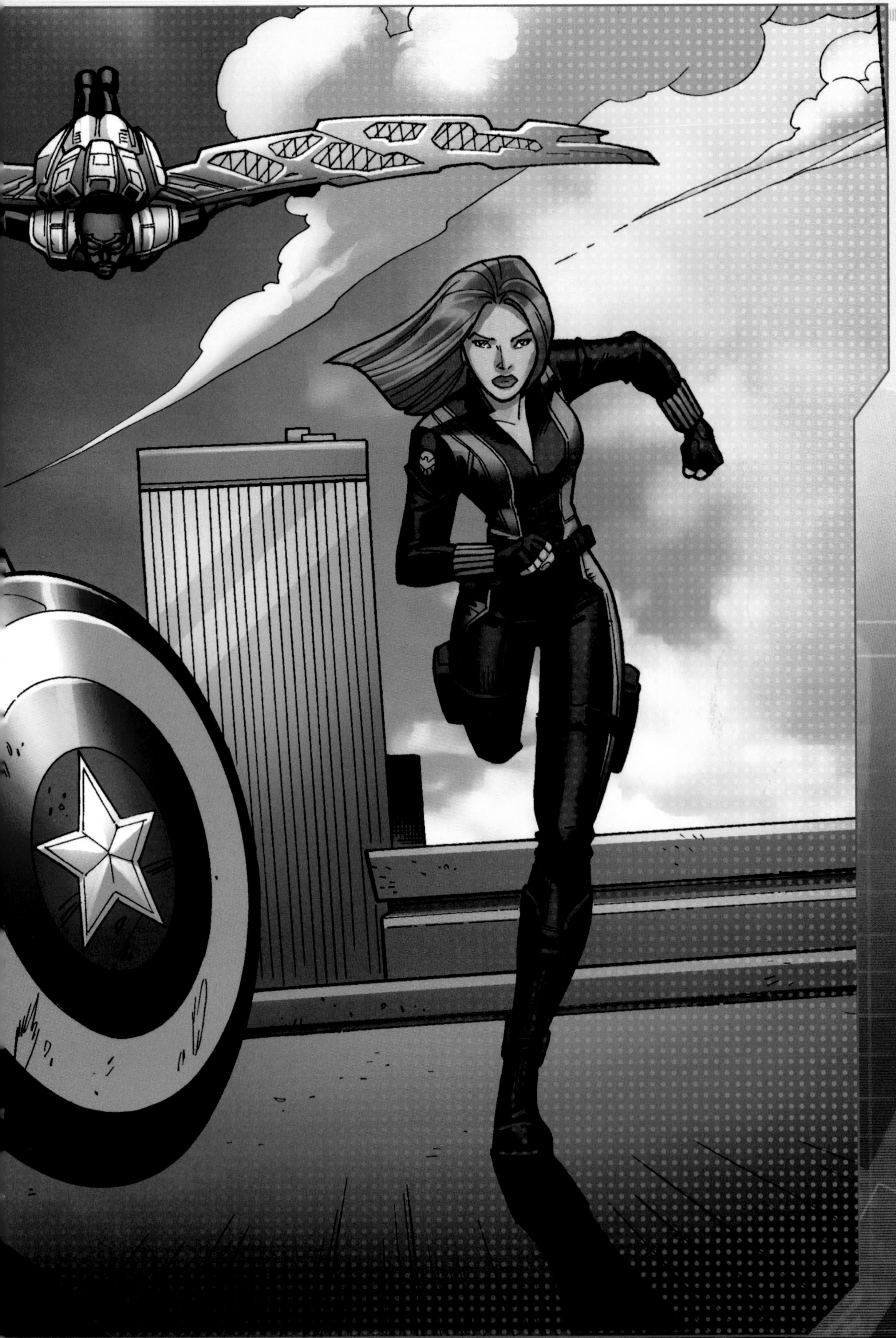

NOTICING THE HELICOPTER'S GUNS WERE AIMED DIRECTLY AT FALCON, Cap tossed his shield at the incoming fire, deflecting the shots. Now realizing it would take something more powerful to destroy Cap's Vibranium shield, the helicopter's pilot started to fly away to regroup. Cap yelled to Falcon to give him a boost up to the copter. They couldn't let it get away.

Falcon grabbed Cap, and they were midair when two more choppers suddenly appeared! One flew straight for Black Widow while the other hovered, the mysterious masked man at the helm! "I'll take him!" Cap shouted. "You get the other one!"

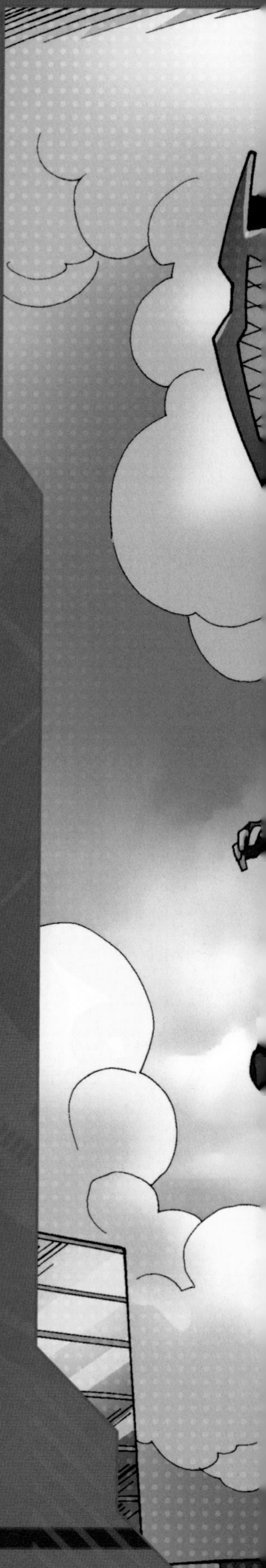

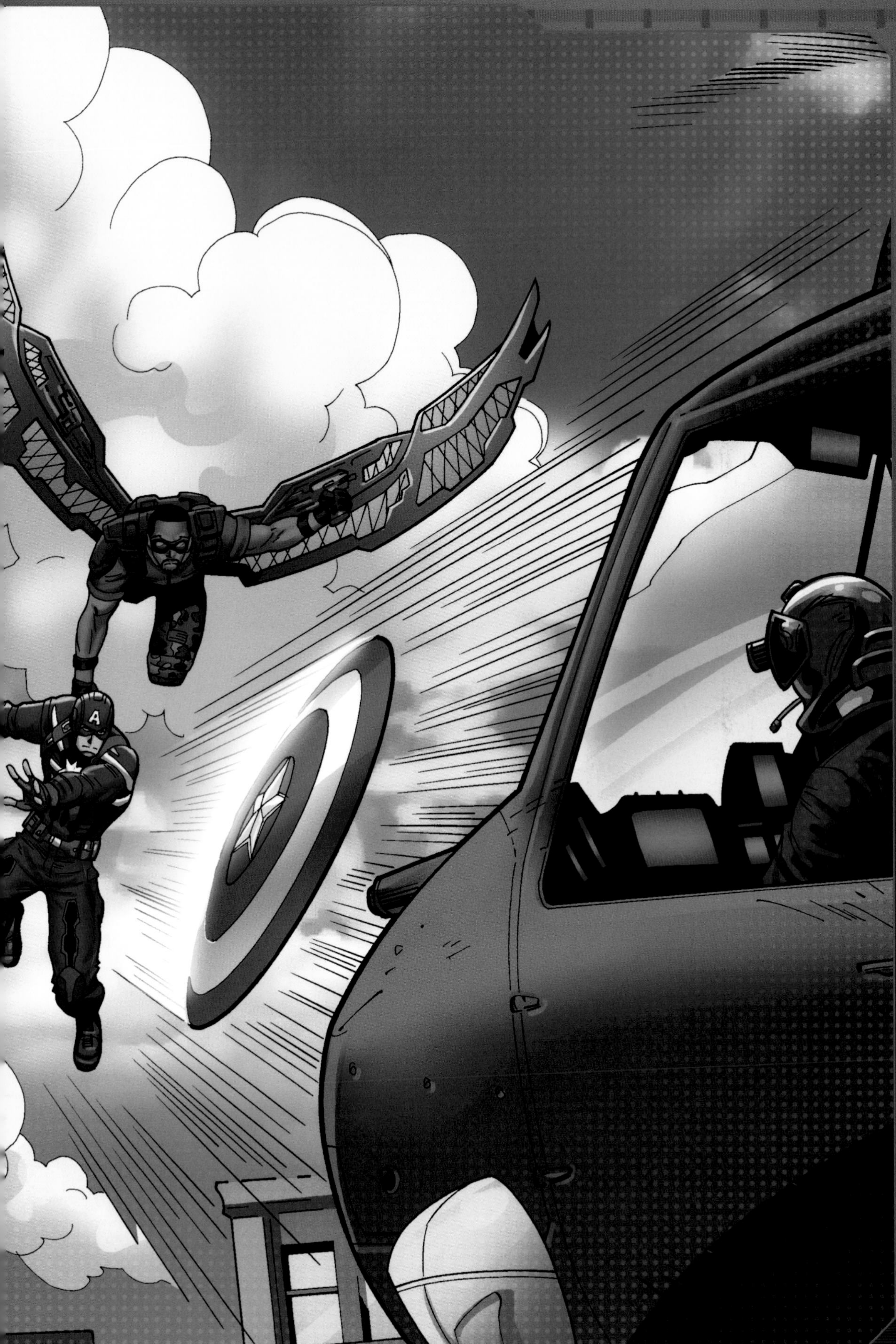

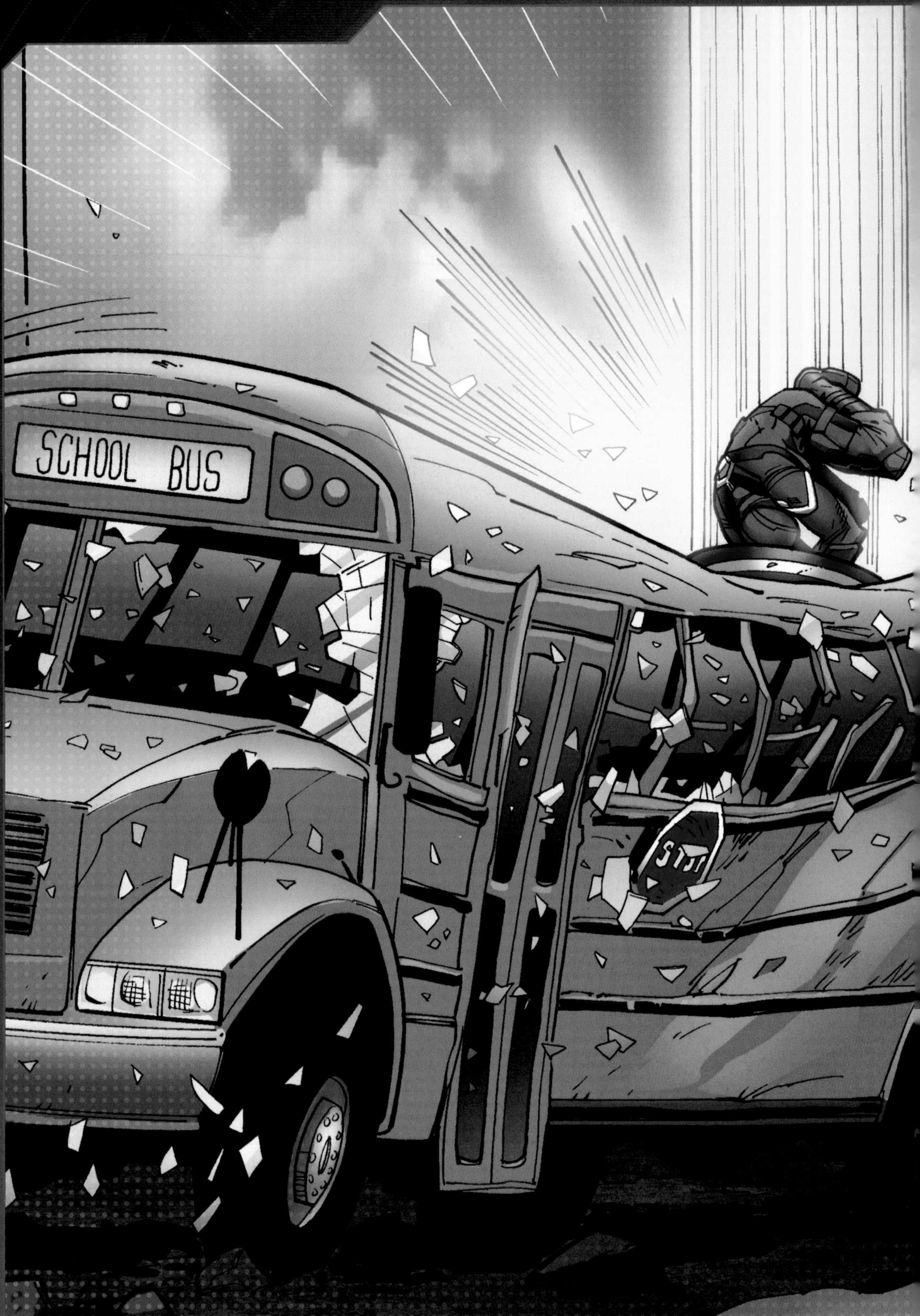
SCHOOL BUS

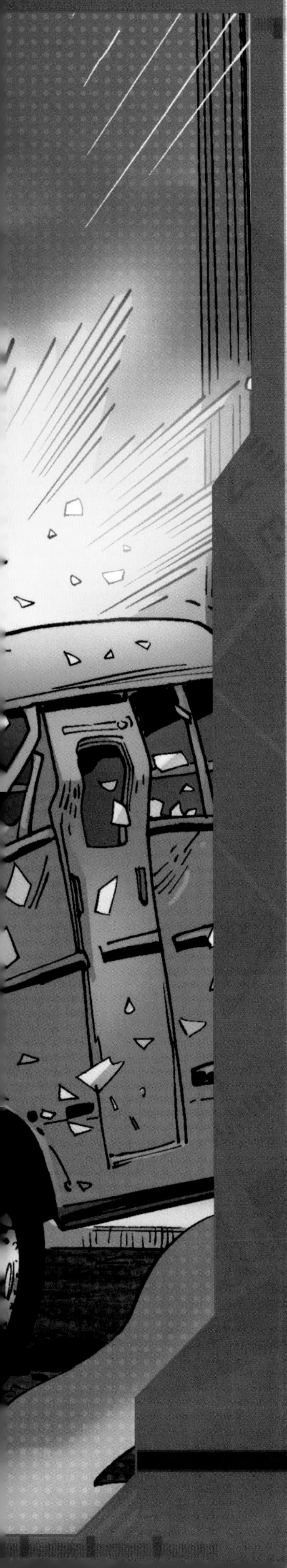

Falcon dropped Captain America into the open door of the helicopter, then flew away to stop the other chopper. "Thank you for bringing S.H.I.E.L.D.'s secrets right to me, Captain America!" the masked man yelled. The Super-Soldier and the Winter Soldier fought in the back of the helicopter. "Too bad I don't have it," Cap taunted. The masked man gave a mighty metal punch to Cap, forcefully knocking him out of the helicopter and into the air!

Cap fell until he crashed through the roof of an empty bus! Determined to find the data drive, the Winter Soldier jumped down after him, shooting at Black Widow with his rocket launcher. She agilely dodged the blast by firing a grappling hook into a freeway overpass, allowing her to swing neatly to the street below.

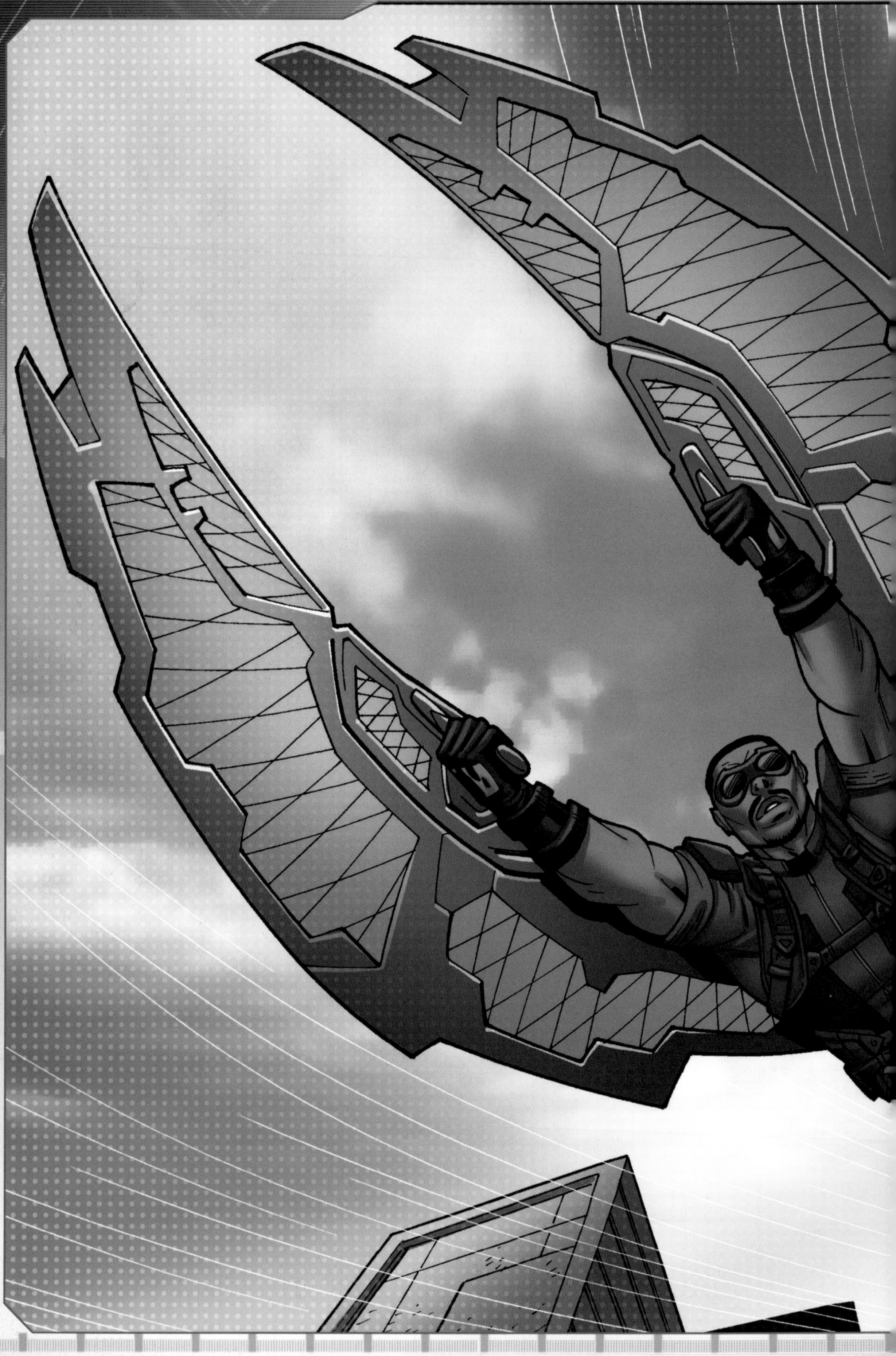

In the sky, Falcon flew after the other helicopter. He had to figure out a way to get it out of the air. He decided to attack like a peregrine falcon would by ZOOMING at top speed toward the copter, causing it to swerve and spin! Falcon's aggressive flying finally forced the helicopter off its course.

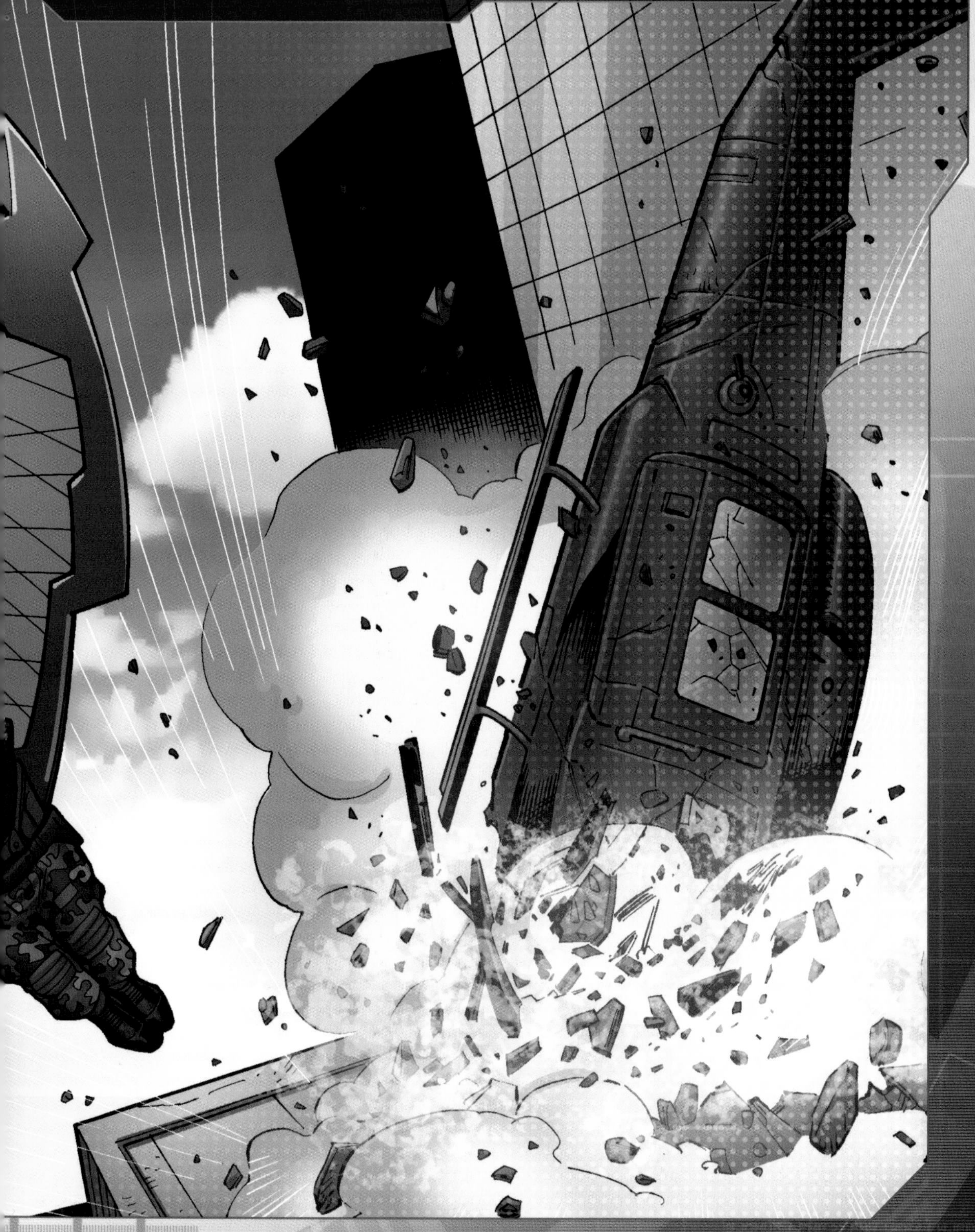

THE OTHER HELICOPTERS LANDED and the mercenaries piled out and met their leader on the ground. The Winter Soldier gave them orders to go after the fallen Super-Soldier, who was still stuck in the bus, while he went after Black Widow. Maybe she has the drive, he thought.

The Winter Soldier vaulted over a concrete barrier, smashing a car roof as he dropped to the street where he had last seen Black Widow. As the masked man scanned the area for her, Black Widow silently crept up and leaped toward him, firing her Widow's Bites! Like a magnet, it stuck to his metal arm, SHOCKING him and momentarily causing the arm to go limp. Puzzled, Winter Soldier studied his useless limb as Black Widow scrambled away, knowing she would need more than just her Widow's Bites to stop this menace.

Back at the bus, Steve sat up, woozy. He had taken quite a fall, but he wasn't very injured. Just then, he heard the CLANK CLANK CLANK of a Gatling gun powering up! Right as the mercenary wielding it was about to press the trigger, Falcon swooped in, knocking over the enemy and the mini gun!

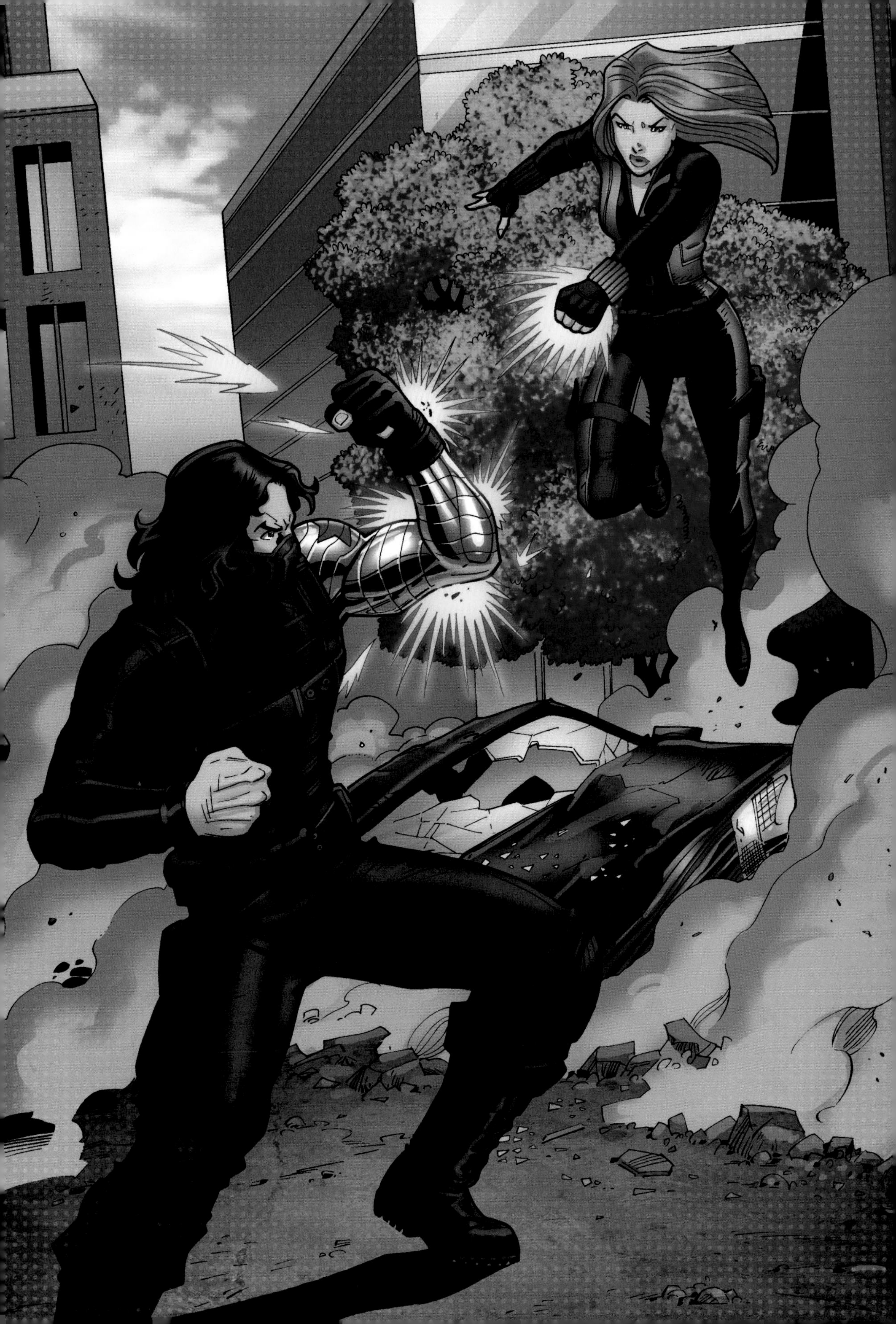

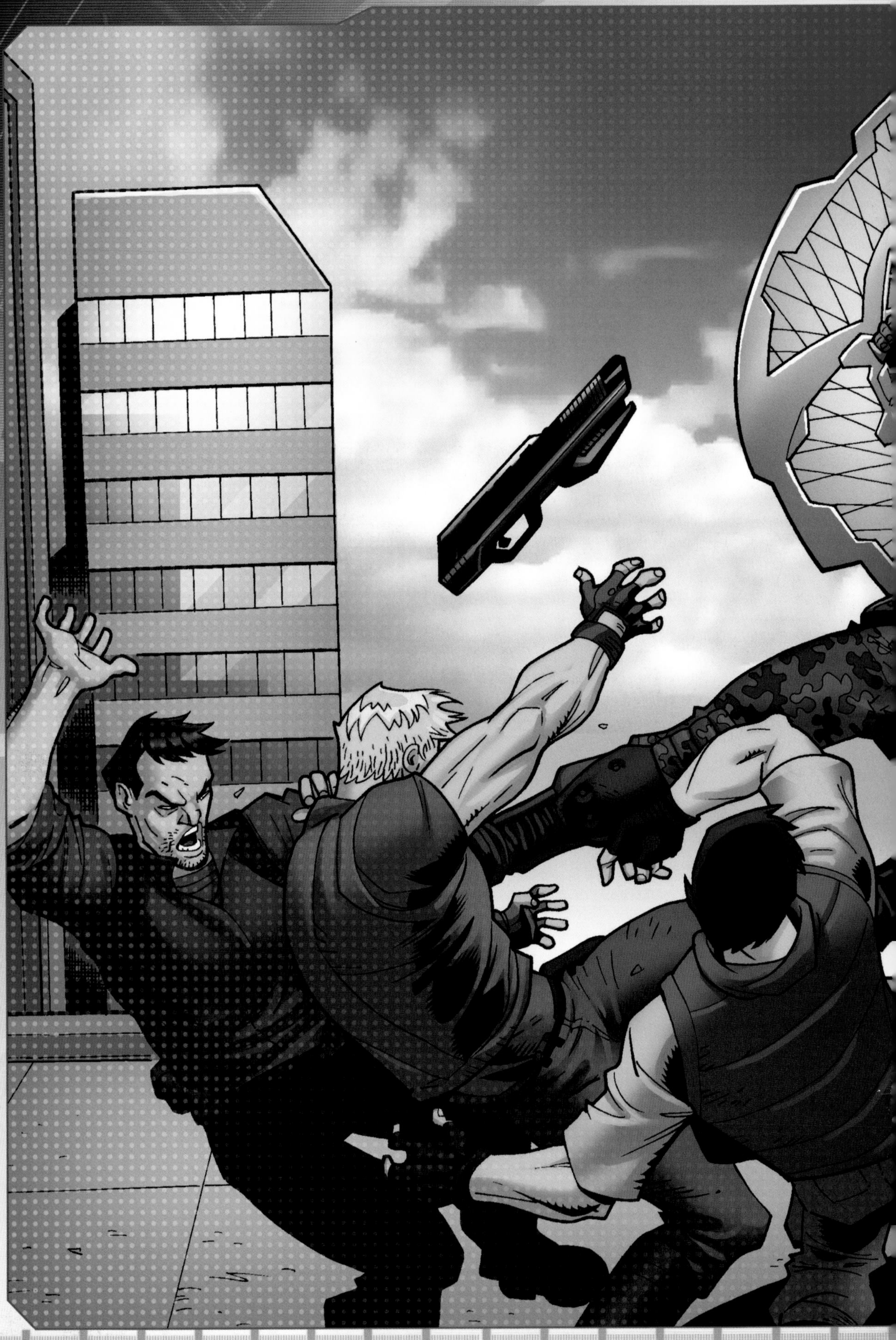

Captain America seized the opportunity to escape from the bus, but he ran right into a brutish merc. He had lost his shield in the fall but saw it in the distance. He'd have to take on this huge guy the old-fashioned way, with a little one-two-punch combo! He slugged away at the thug, dazing him but not knocking him over—until Falcon swooped in with a double kick, knocking the big man off his feet! Cap thanked Falcon as he grabbed his shield, but there was no time for rest.

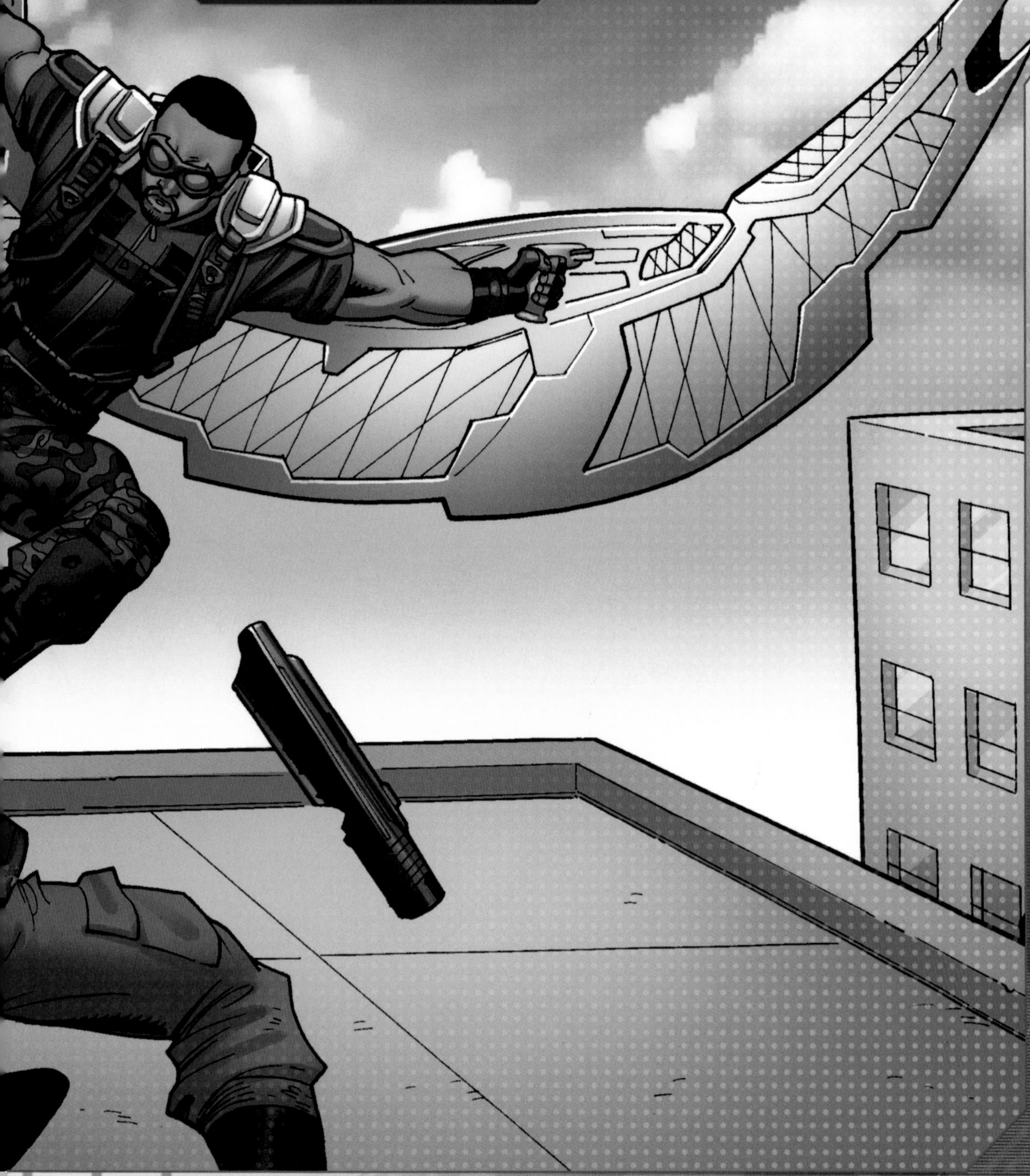

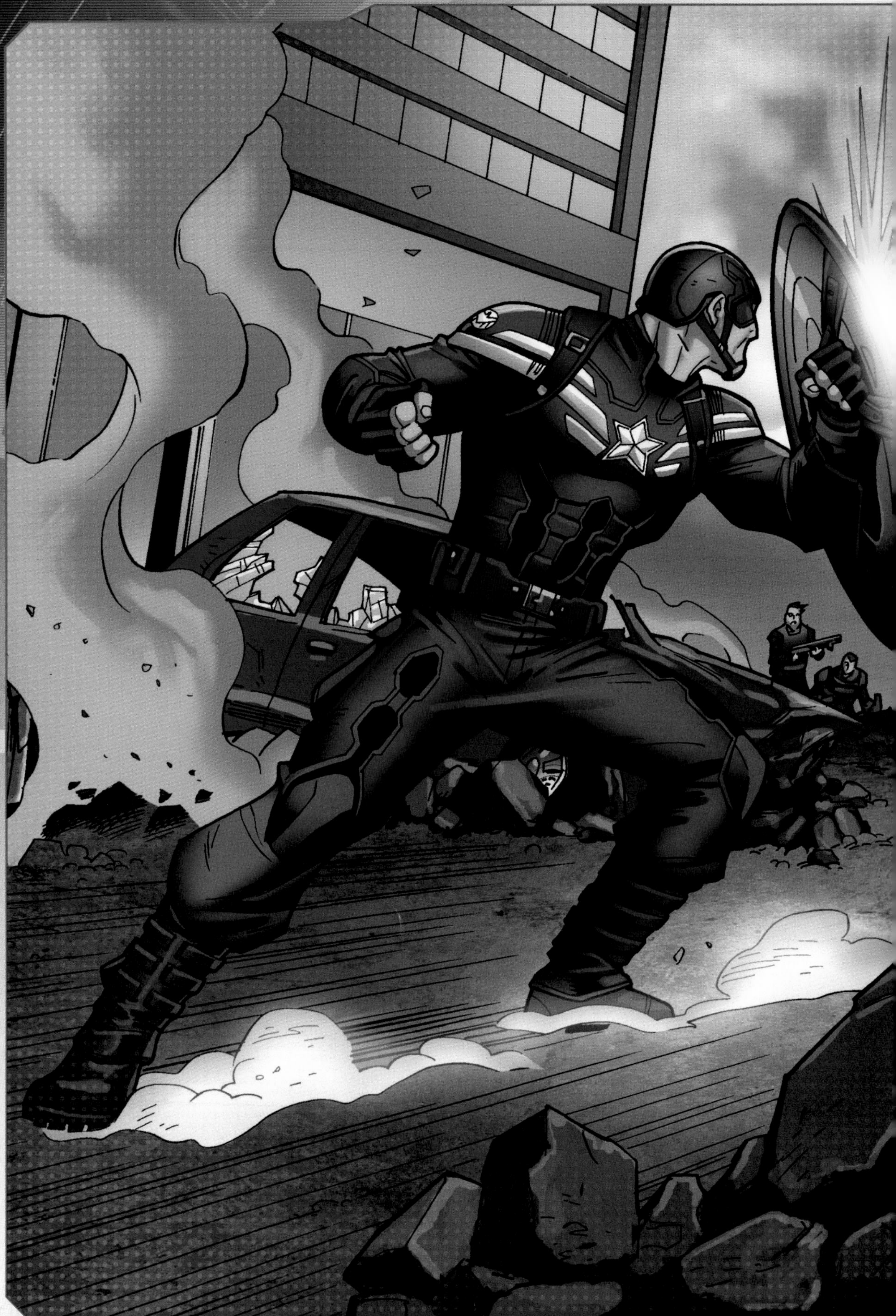

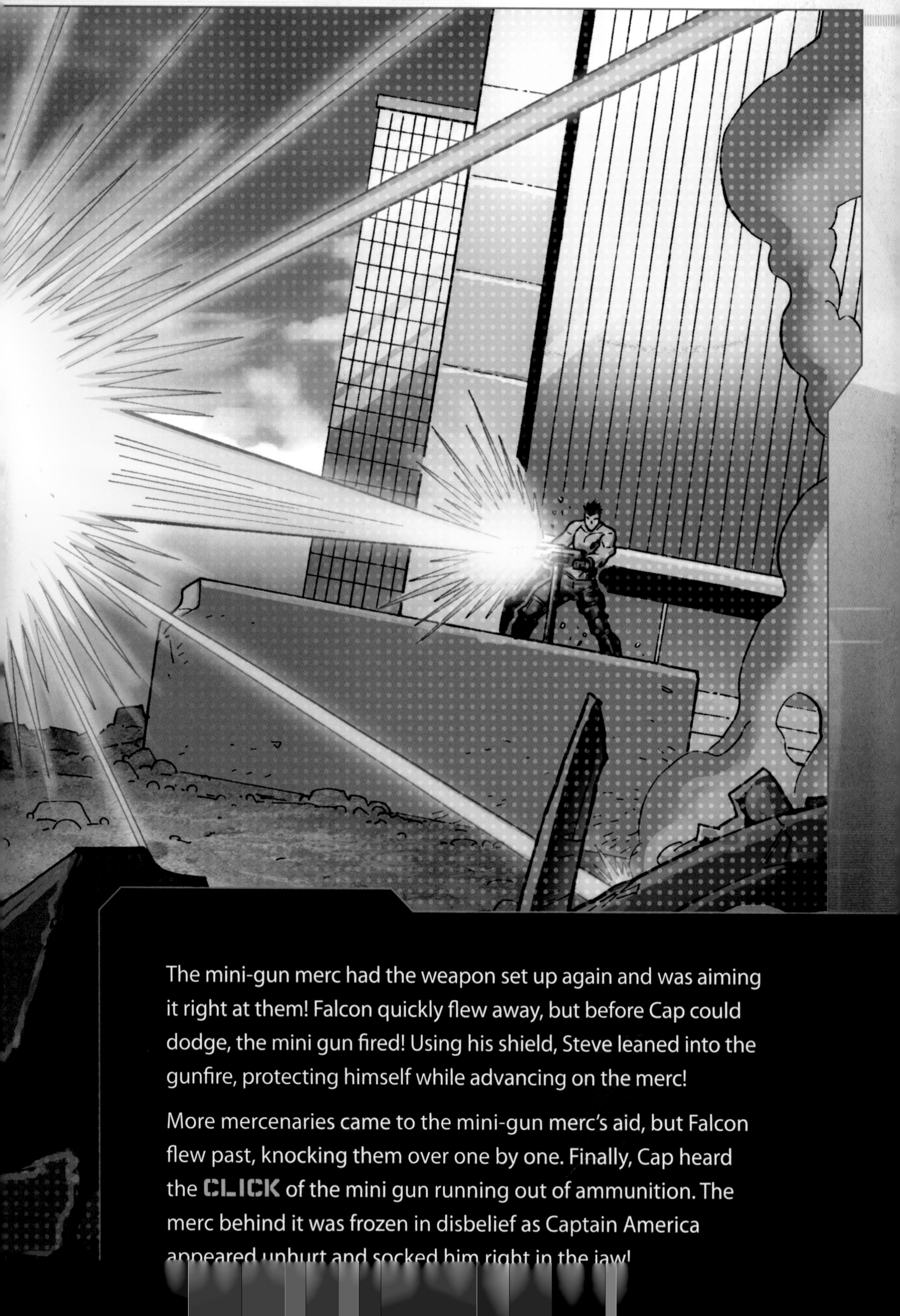

The mini-gun merc had the weapon set up again and was aiming it right at them! Falcon quickly flew away, but before Cap could dodge, the mini gun fired! Using his shield, Steve leaned into the gunfire, protecting himself while advancing on the merc!

More mercenaries came to the mini-gun merc's aid, but Falcon flew past, knocking them over one by one. Finally, Cap heard the **CLICK** of the mini gun running out of ammunition. The merc behind it was frozen in disbelief as Captain America appeared unhurt and socked him right in the jaw!

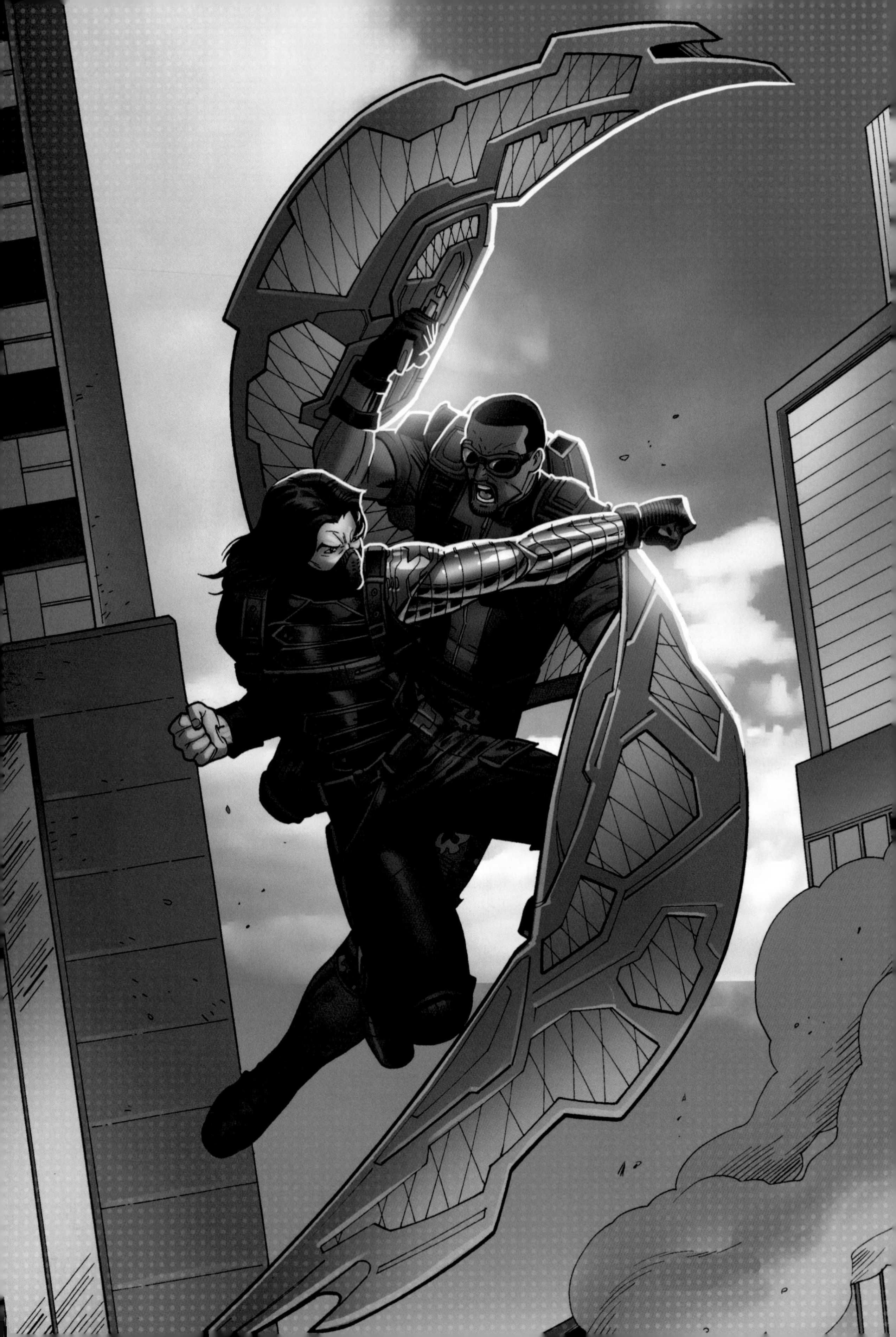

WITH CAP UNDER PRESSURE from the Gatling gun and Black Widow nearby battling some mercenaries with an assault of kicks and punches, Falcon had seen an opportunity to take out the Winter Soldier. He swooped down at an incredible speed and clashed into the metal-armed assassin! Falcon's wings grasped the Winter Soldier and the two became entangled.

"Give me the data drive!" the Winter Soldier yelled.

"Wish I could help you there," Falcon responded. "That metal arm get hot in the sun?" he teased. They wrestled back and forth until finally Falcon broke free and shot back into the sky. *He sure is strong,* Falcon thought. *And he can't take a joke.*

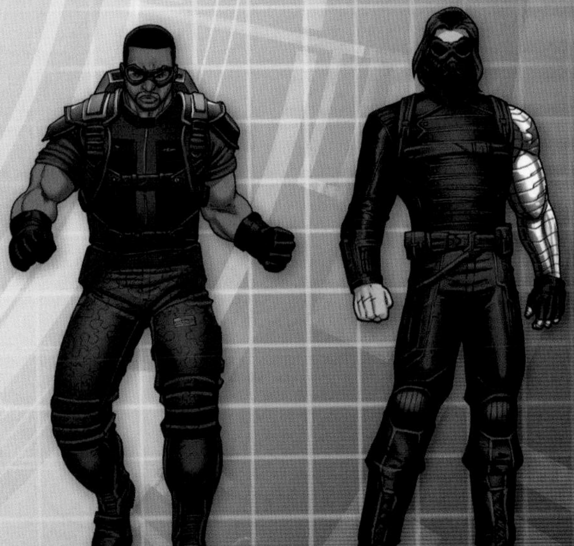

With one group of thugs taken care of but more approaching, Cap spied the Winter Soldier, who had turned his attention back to Black Widow. Circling the skies, Falcon shouted down to Captain America as he dove to battle more goons, "Go! I got this!" Cap took off running as Winter Soldier fired his rocket launcher at Black Widow.

EXPLOSIONS surrounded Black Widow as she jumped and flipped over abandoned cars. Right as the Winter Soldier took aim again, Captain America launched himself through the air toward the masked man.

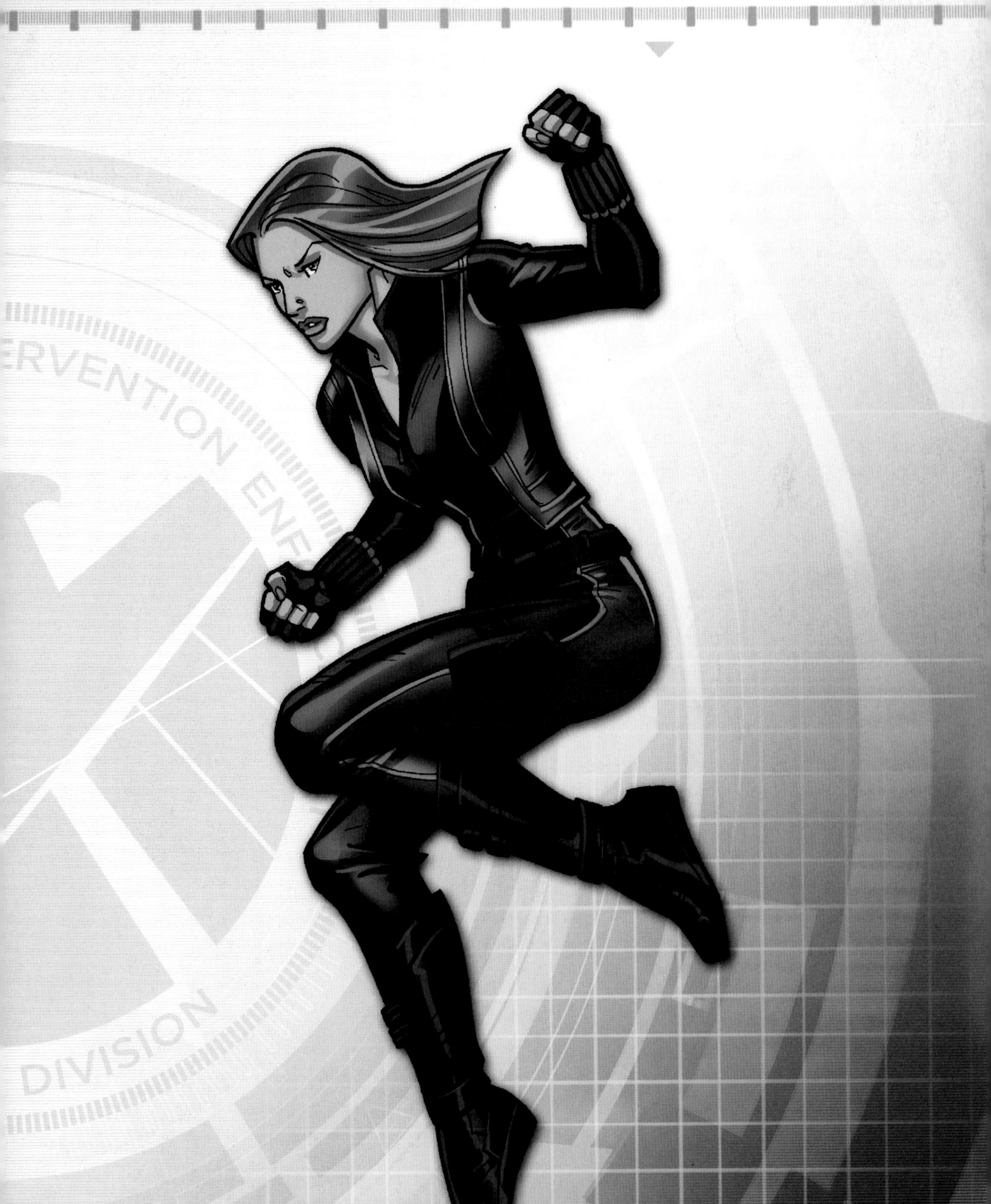
ERVENTION ENF
DIVISION

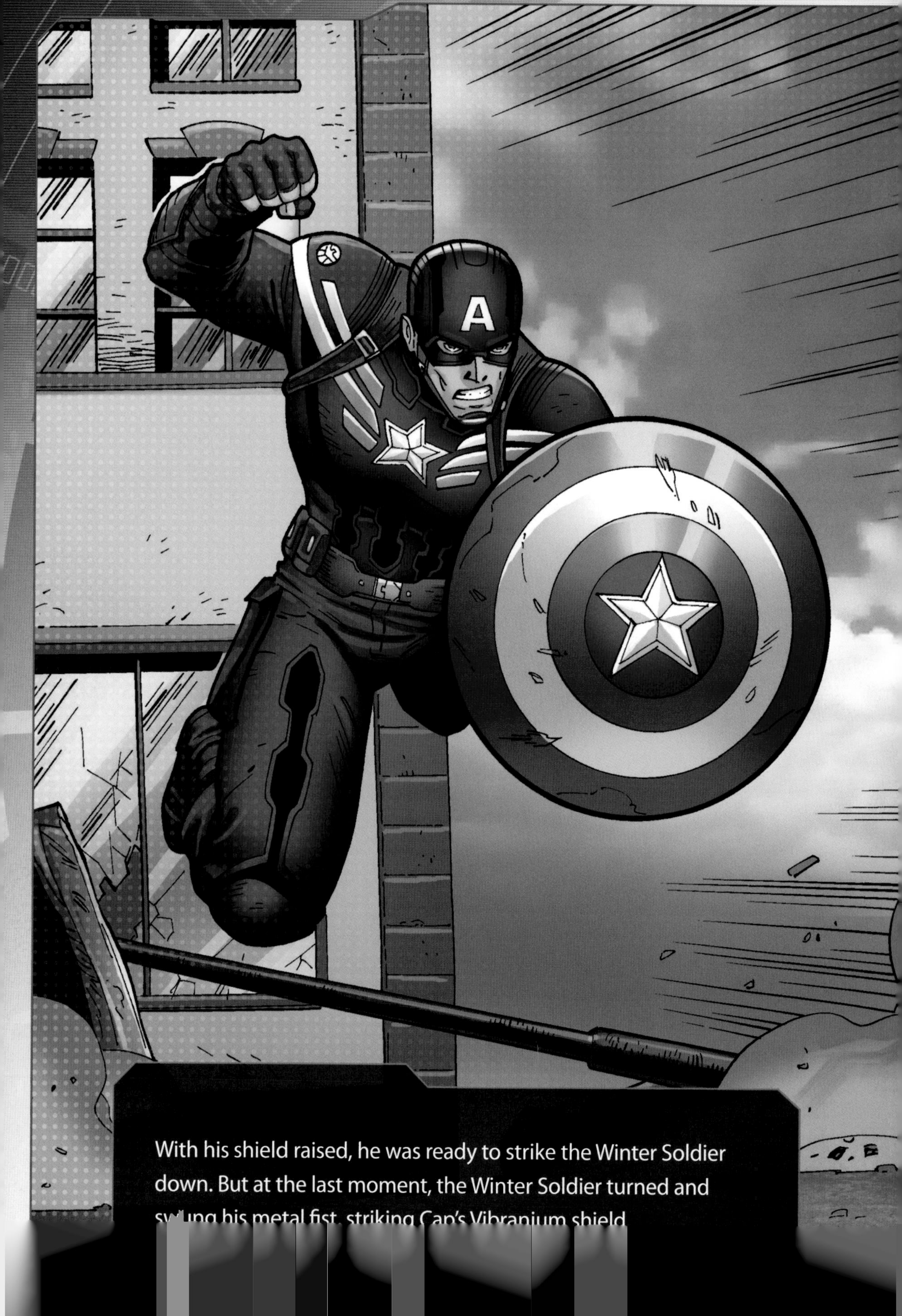

With his shield raised, he was ready to strike the Winter Soldier down. But at the last moment, the Winter Soldier turned and swung his metal fist, striking Cap's Vibranium shield.

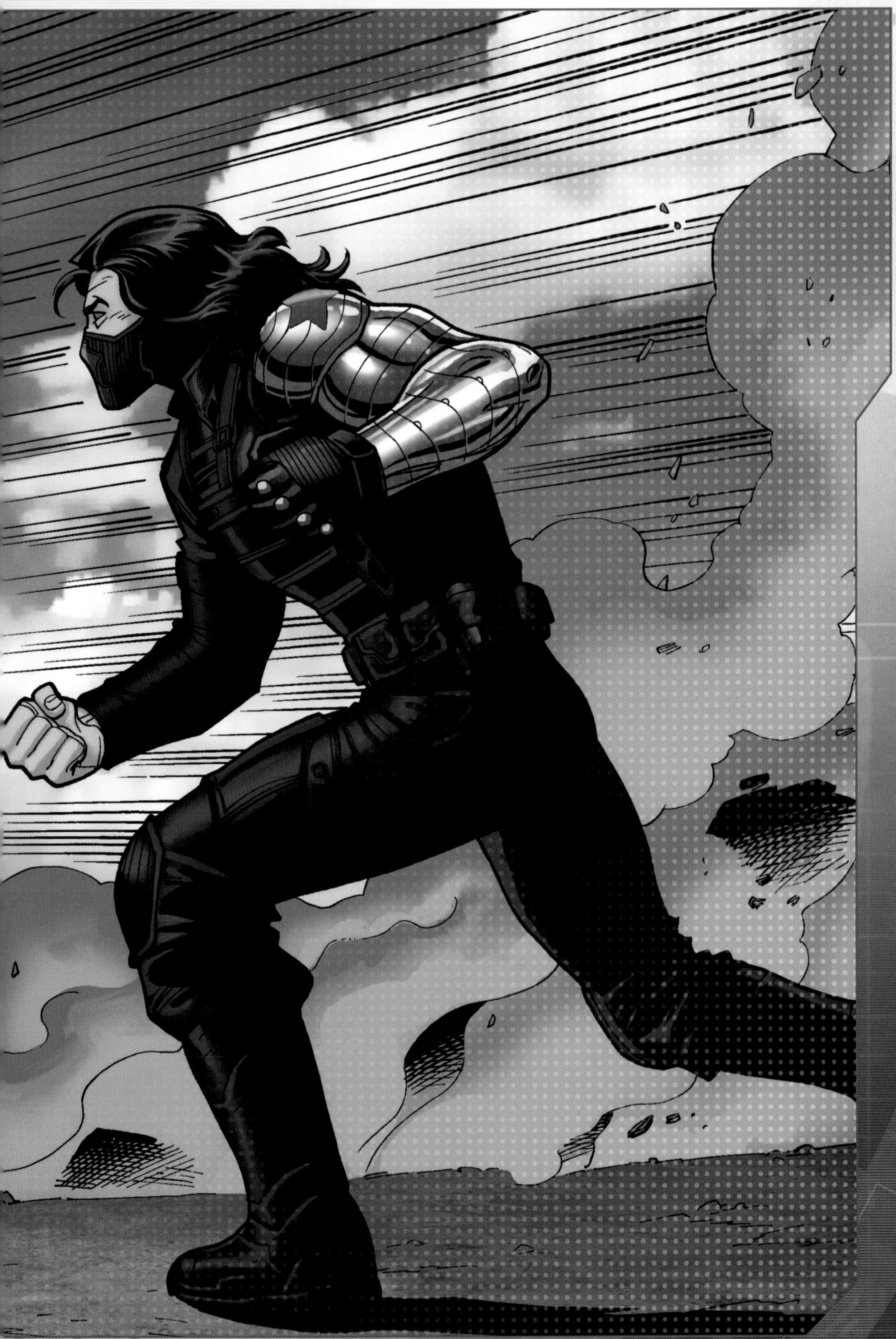

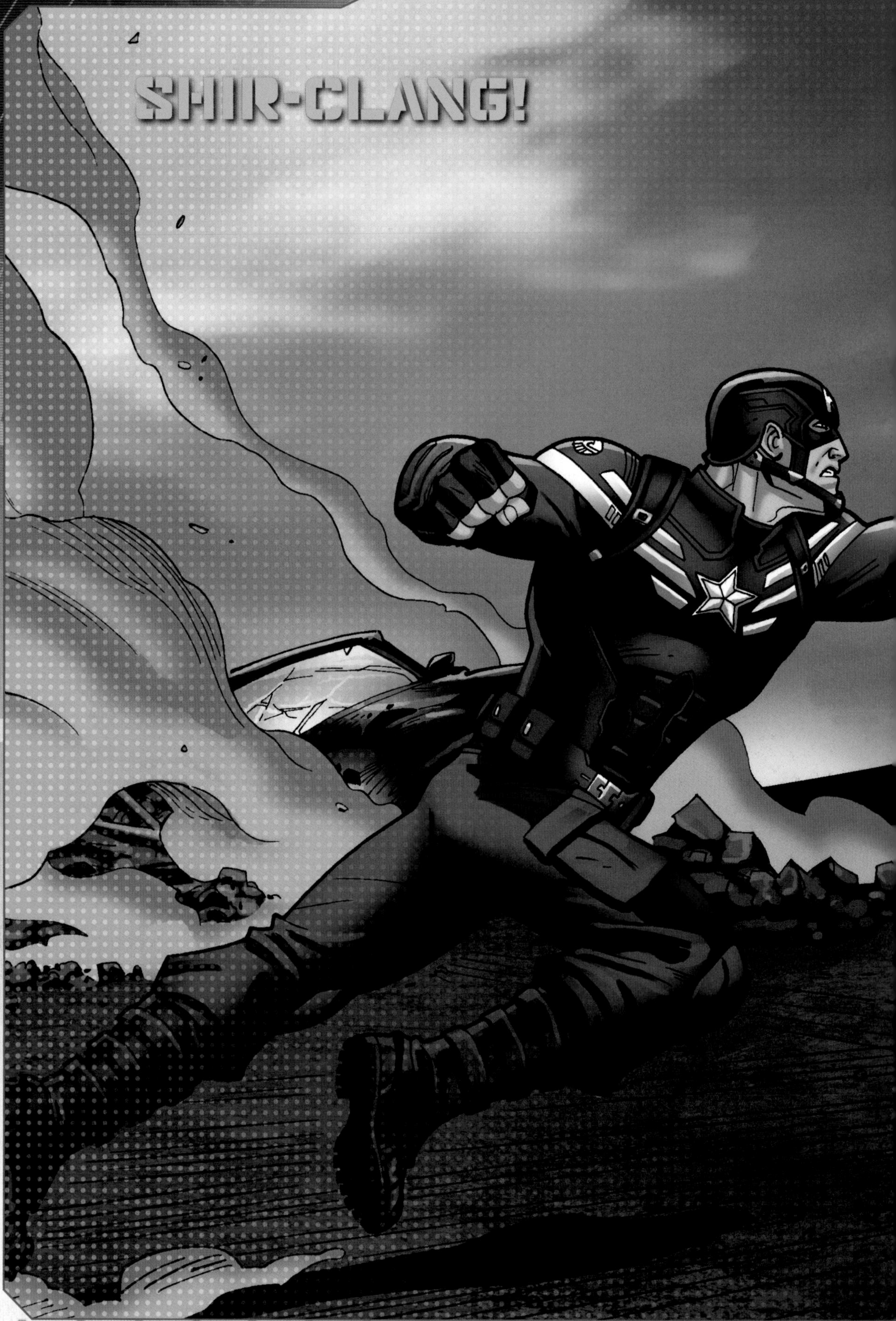
SHIR-CLANG!

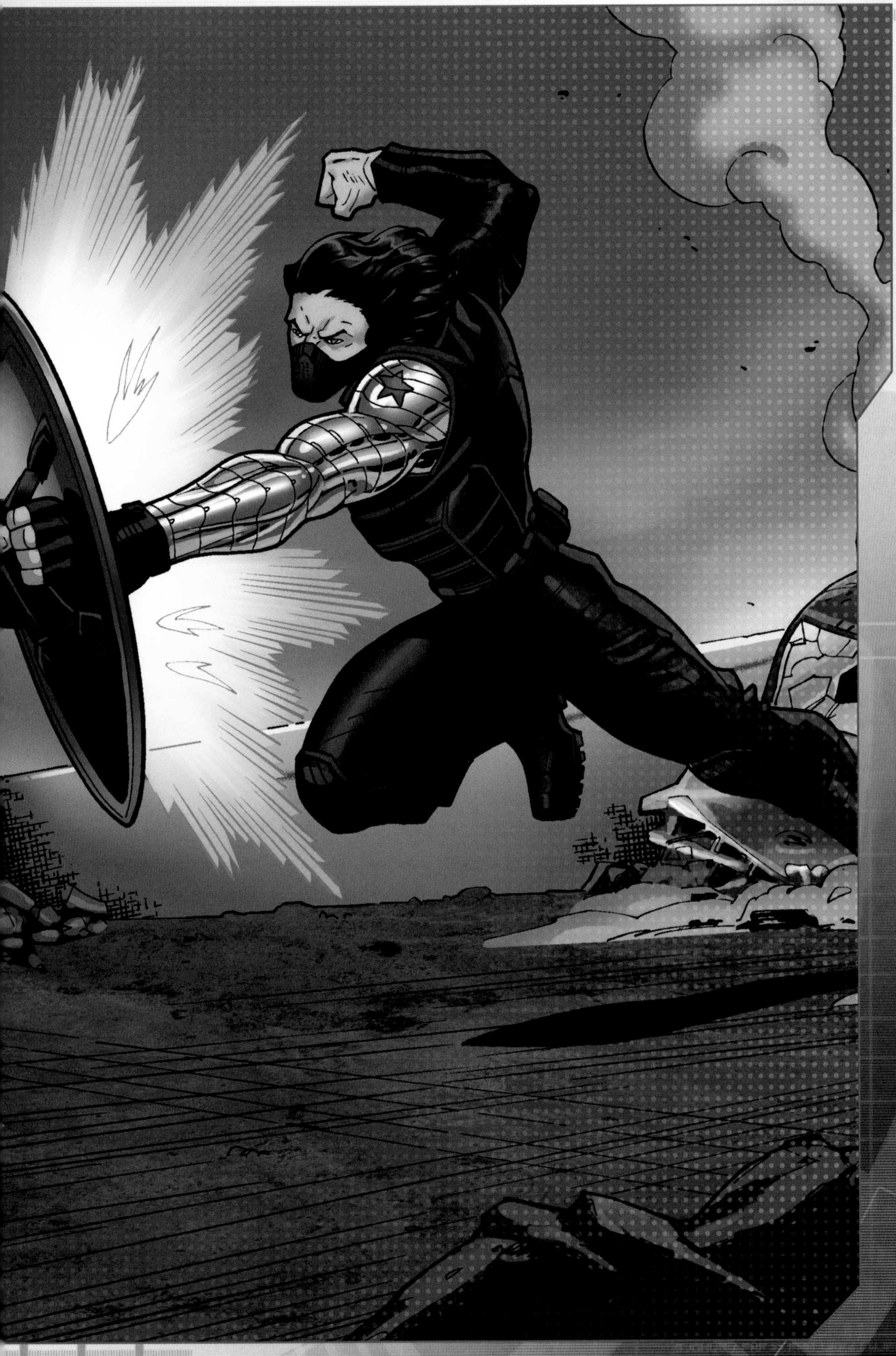

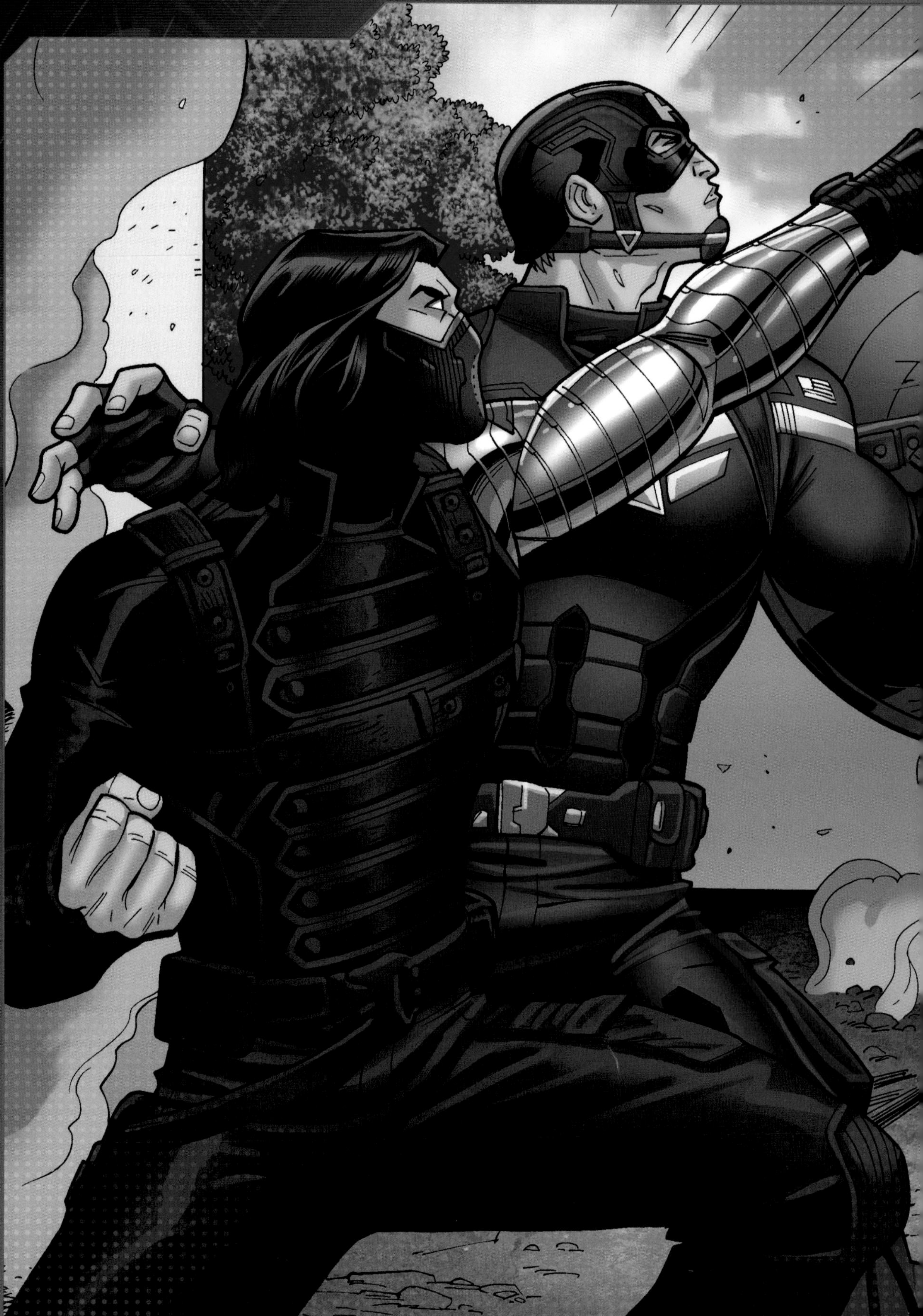

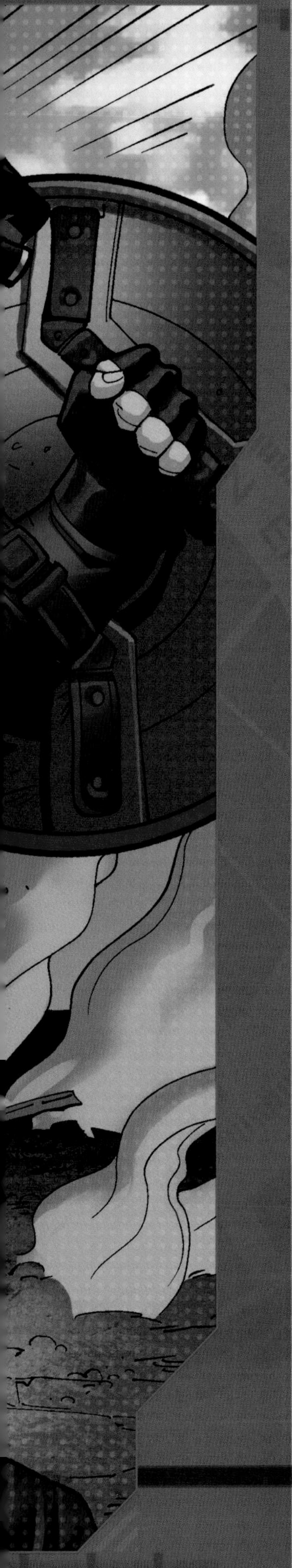

THE IMPACT THREW BOTH OF THEM BACK! Recovering quickly, the Winter Soldier fired his rocket launcher at Cap, who blocked the rocket with his shield.

CLANG! The missile bounced off the red, white, and blue Vibranium star, exploding on the concrete.

Frustrated, the Winter Soldier discarded the launcher and rushed at Steve, this time using quick and furious punches.

9022-RFJ_021-32_LM45

KTL_0-4T3U-R9-L2_GFL2

00_T8-2044T9_00-KJS-0

Cap fought back, landing punch after punch. This is for Fury, Steve thought as he whaled away.

Steve beat him with crippling hits to the body and shots to the face, which loosened the Winter Soldier's mask.

Cap then flipped Winter Soldier, sending him crashing to the ground. Captain America looked at his hand and realized he had ripped the assassin's mask off in the fight.

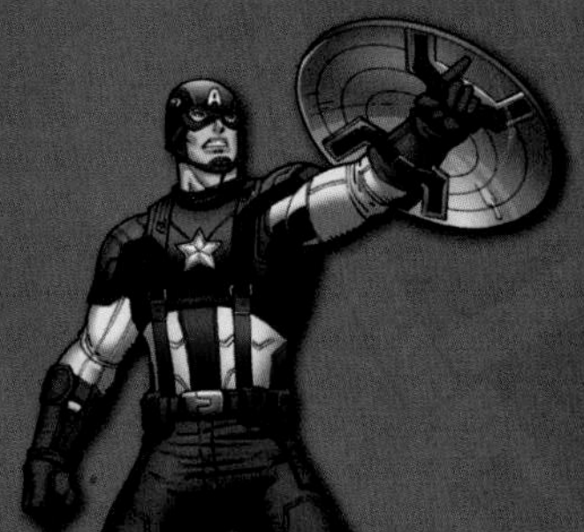

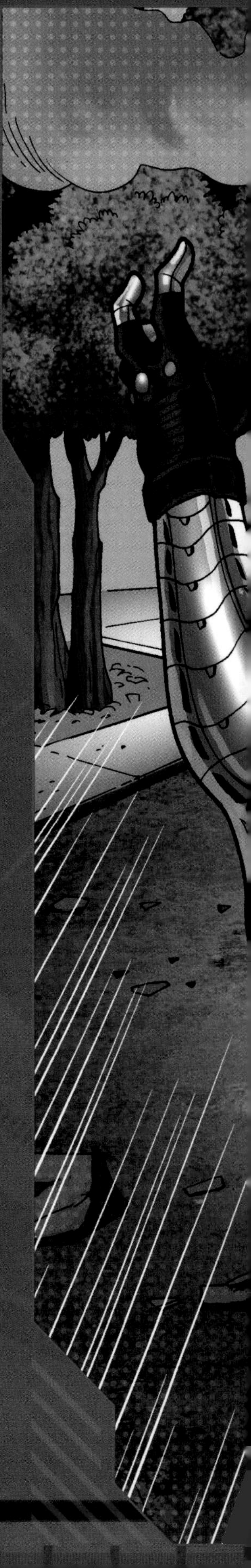

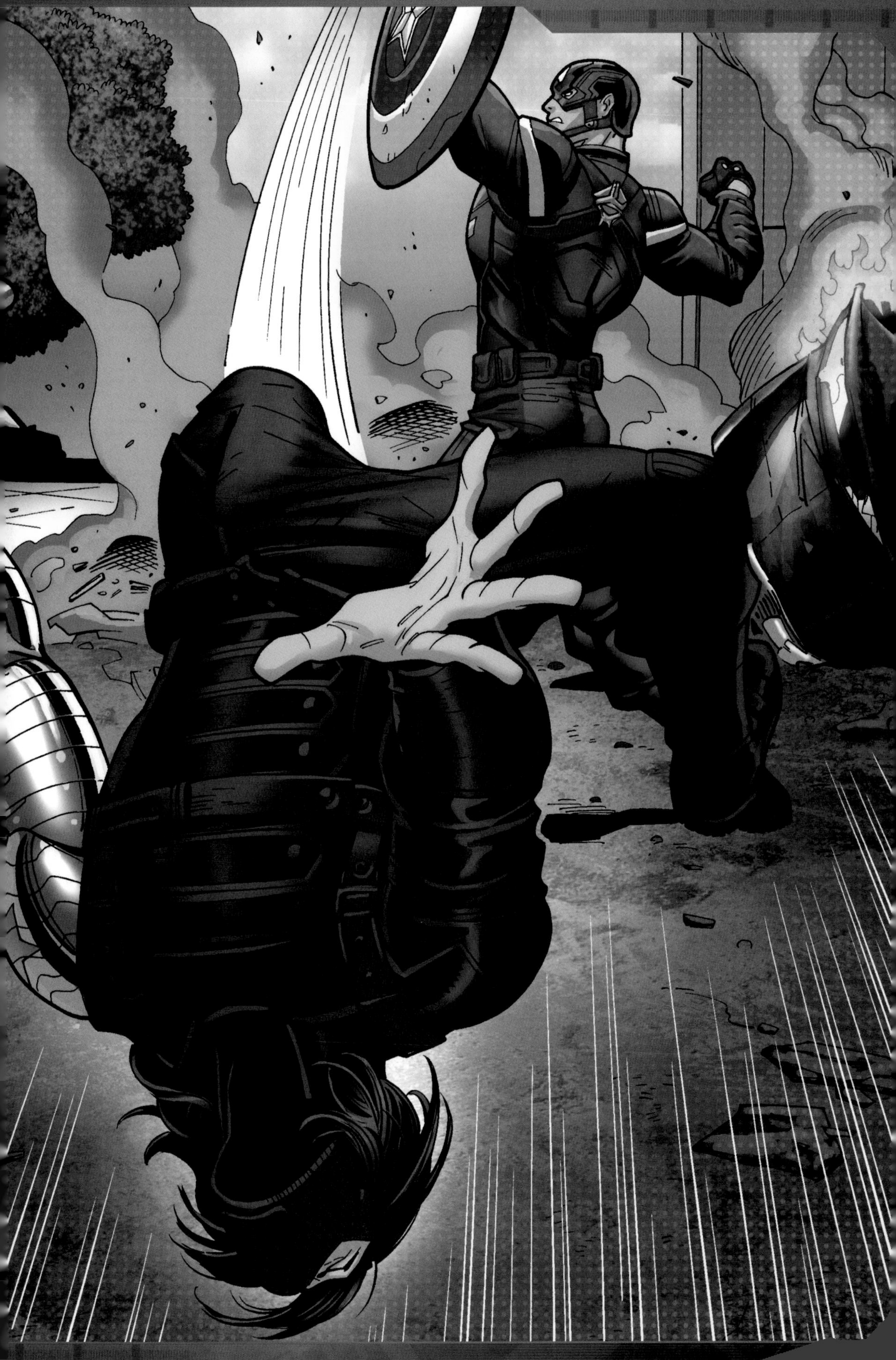

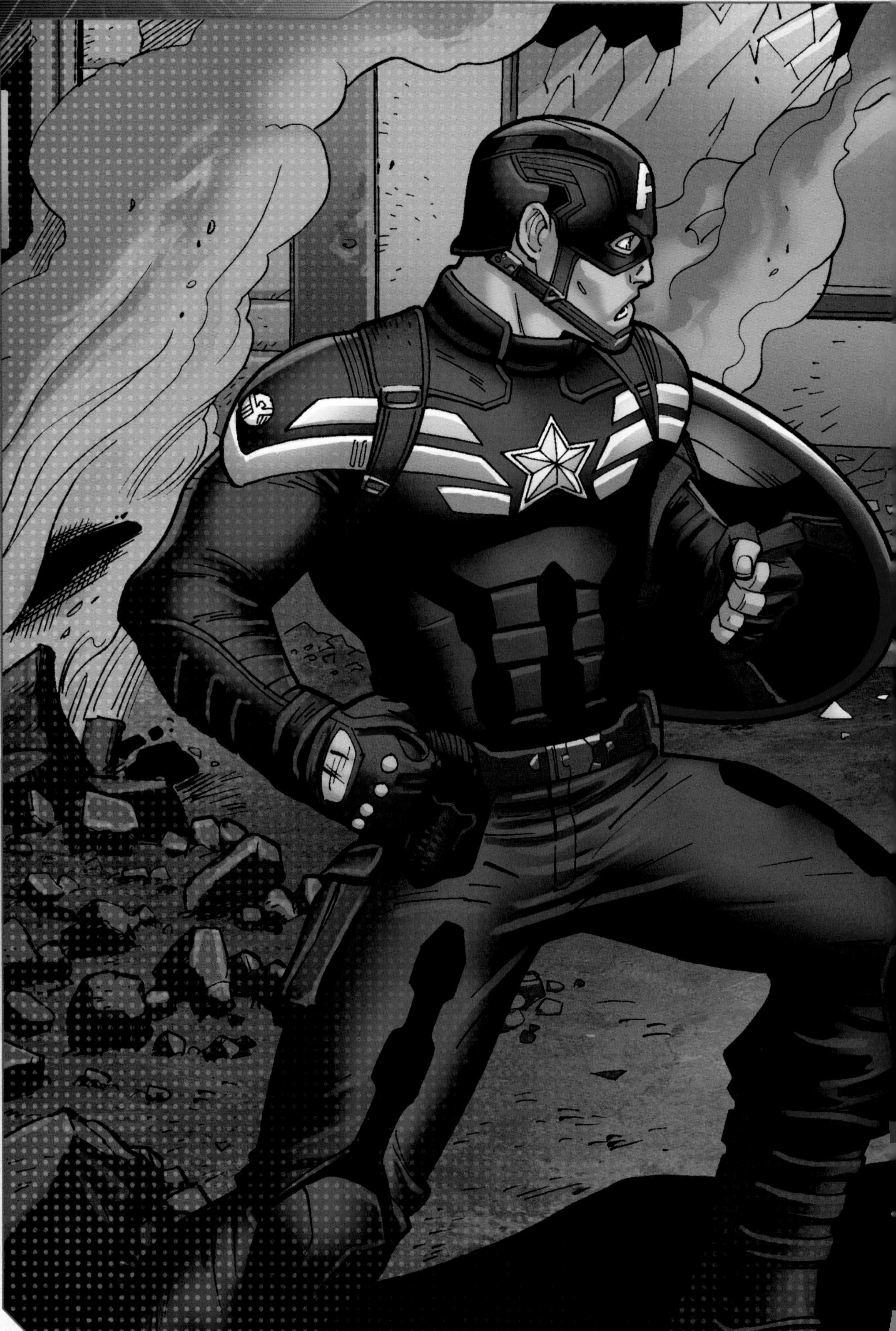

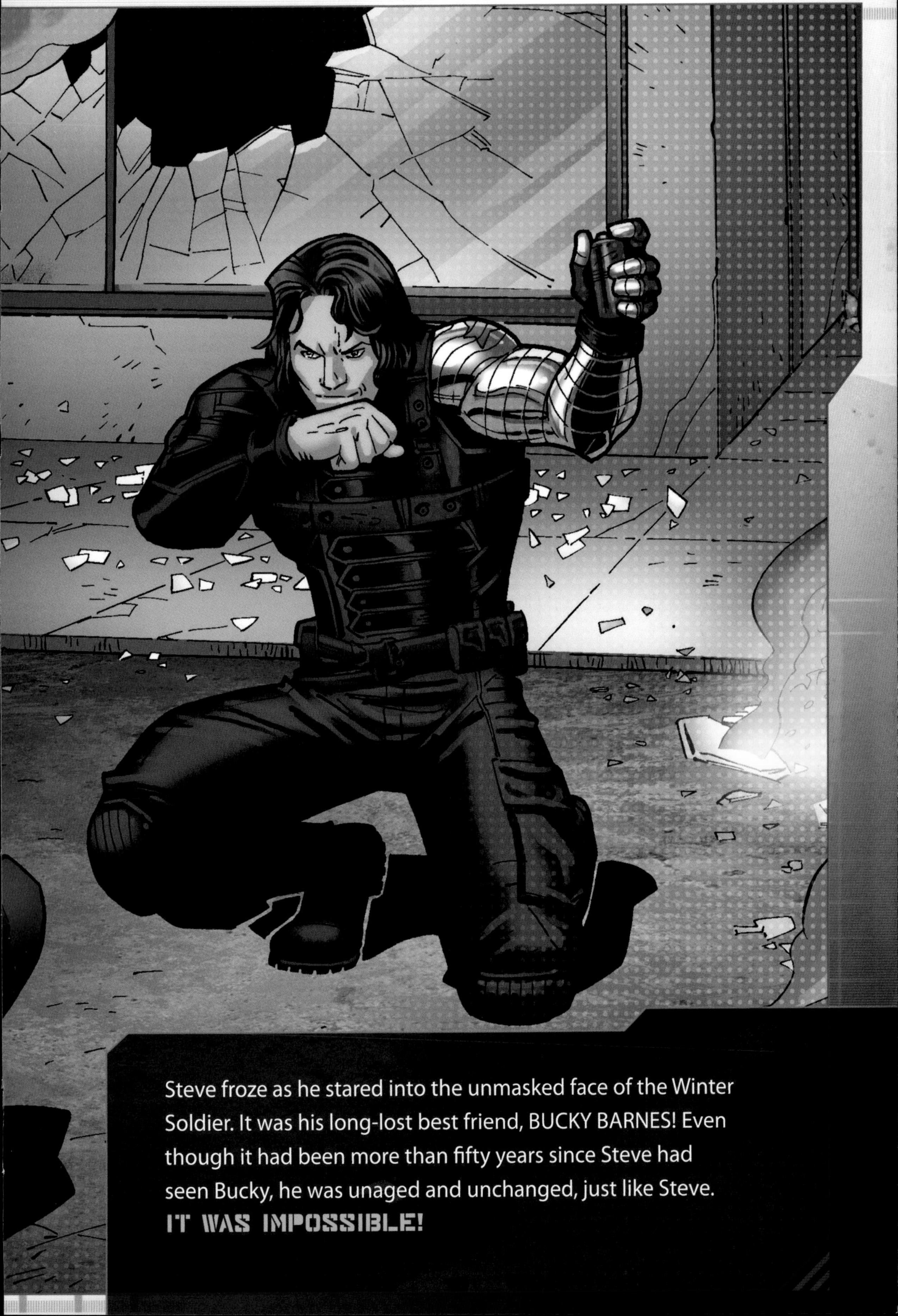

Steve froze as he stared into the unmasked face of the Winter Soldier. It was his long-lost best friend, BUCKY BARNES! Even though it had been more than fifty years since Steve had seen Bucky, he was unaged and unchanged, just like Steve.

IT WAS IMPOSSIBLE!

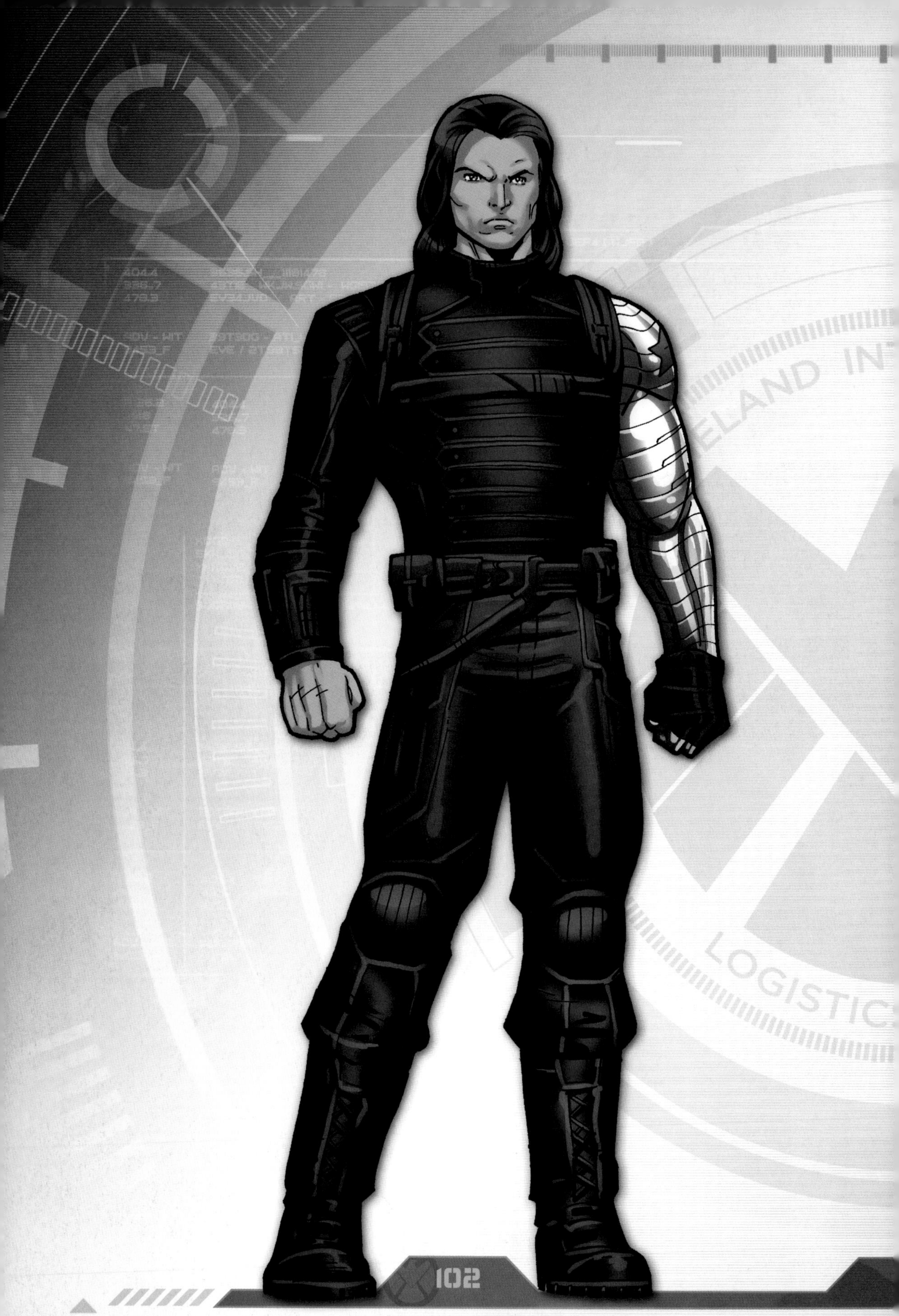

"**BUCKY?**" Steve asked, wondering if his friend recognized him. "Who the heck is Bucky?" the Winter Soldier shot back.

Steve lowered his shield, shocked that his friend was still alive. The Winter Soldier used this opportunity to grab a hidden laser pistol from behind his back, pulling the trigger on Steve.

WHOOSH! Falcon swooped from the sky, throwing Bucky's aim off. The shot narrowly missed Steve's head.

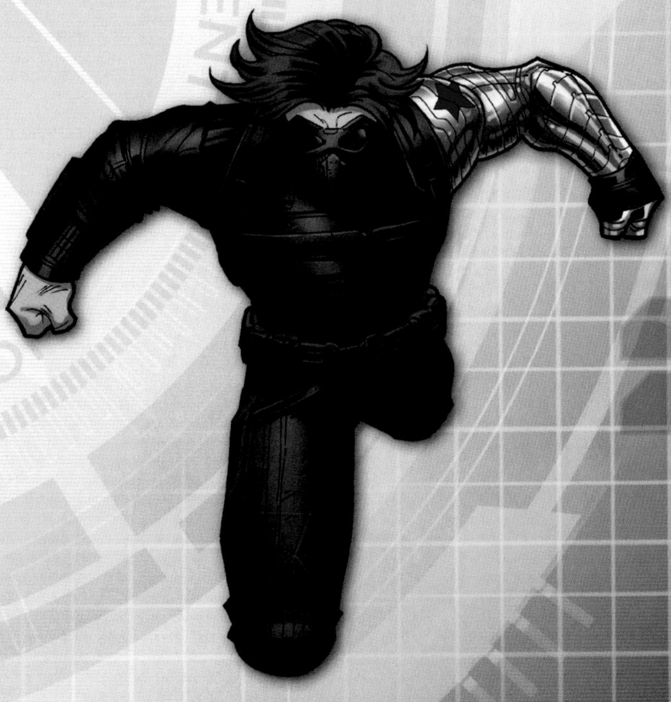

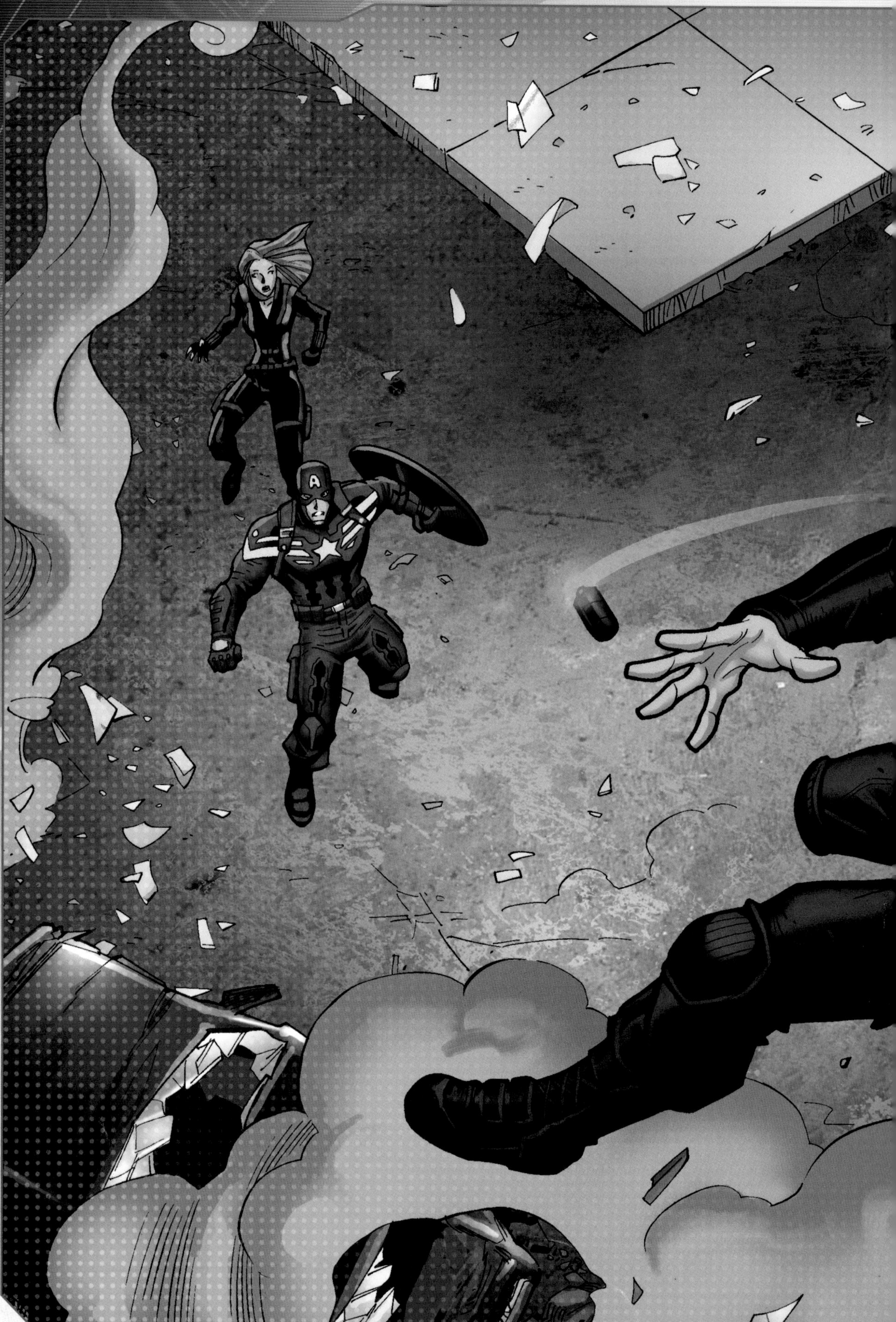

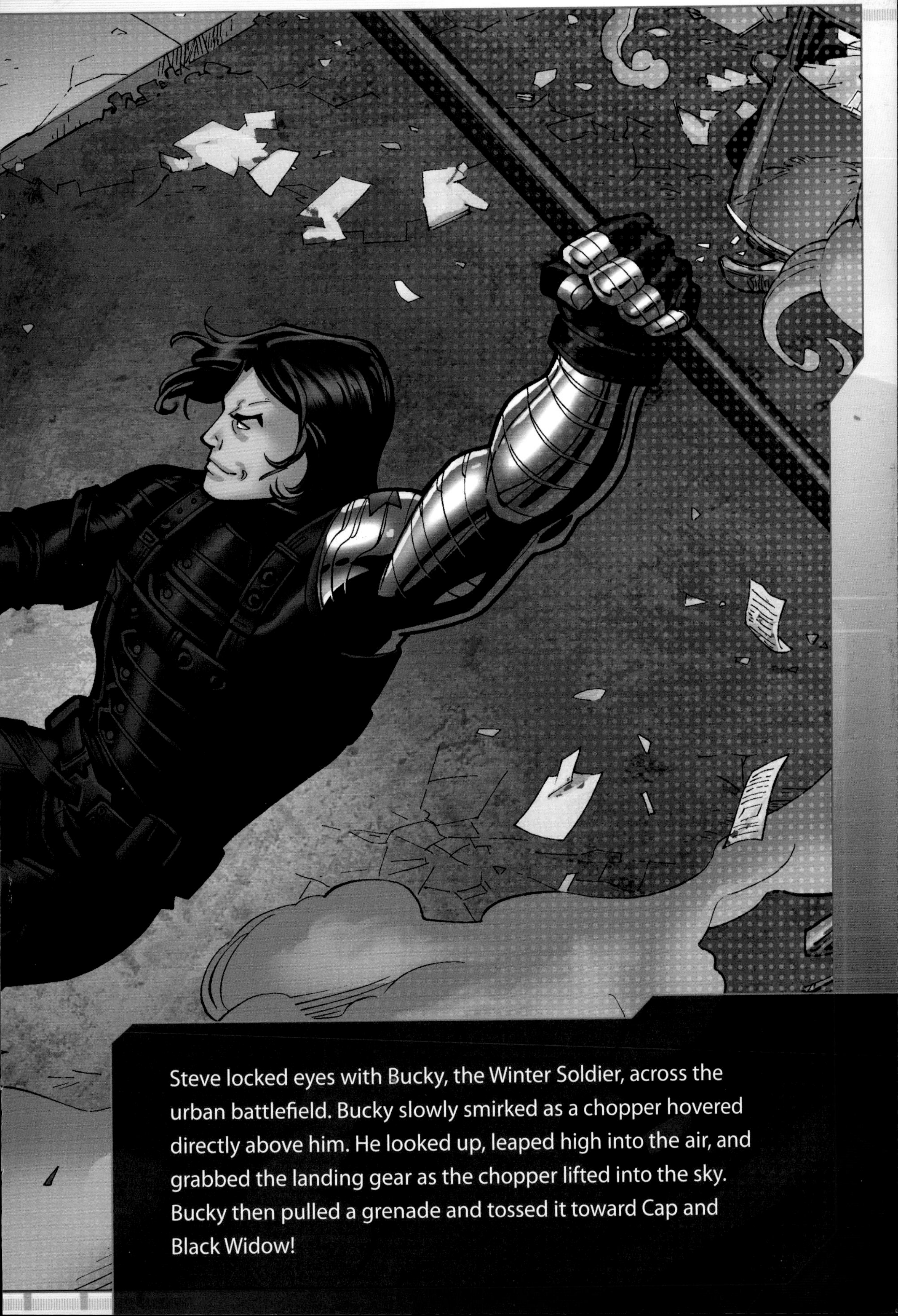

Steve locked eyes with Bucky, the Winter Soldier, across the urban battlefield. Bucky slowly smirked as a chopper hovered directly above him. He looked up, leaped high into the air, and grabbed the landing gear as the chopper lifted into the sky. Bucky then pulled a grenade and tossed it toward Cap and Black Widow!

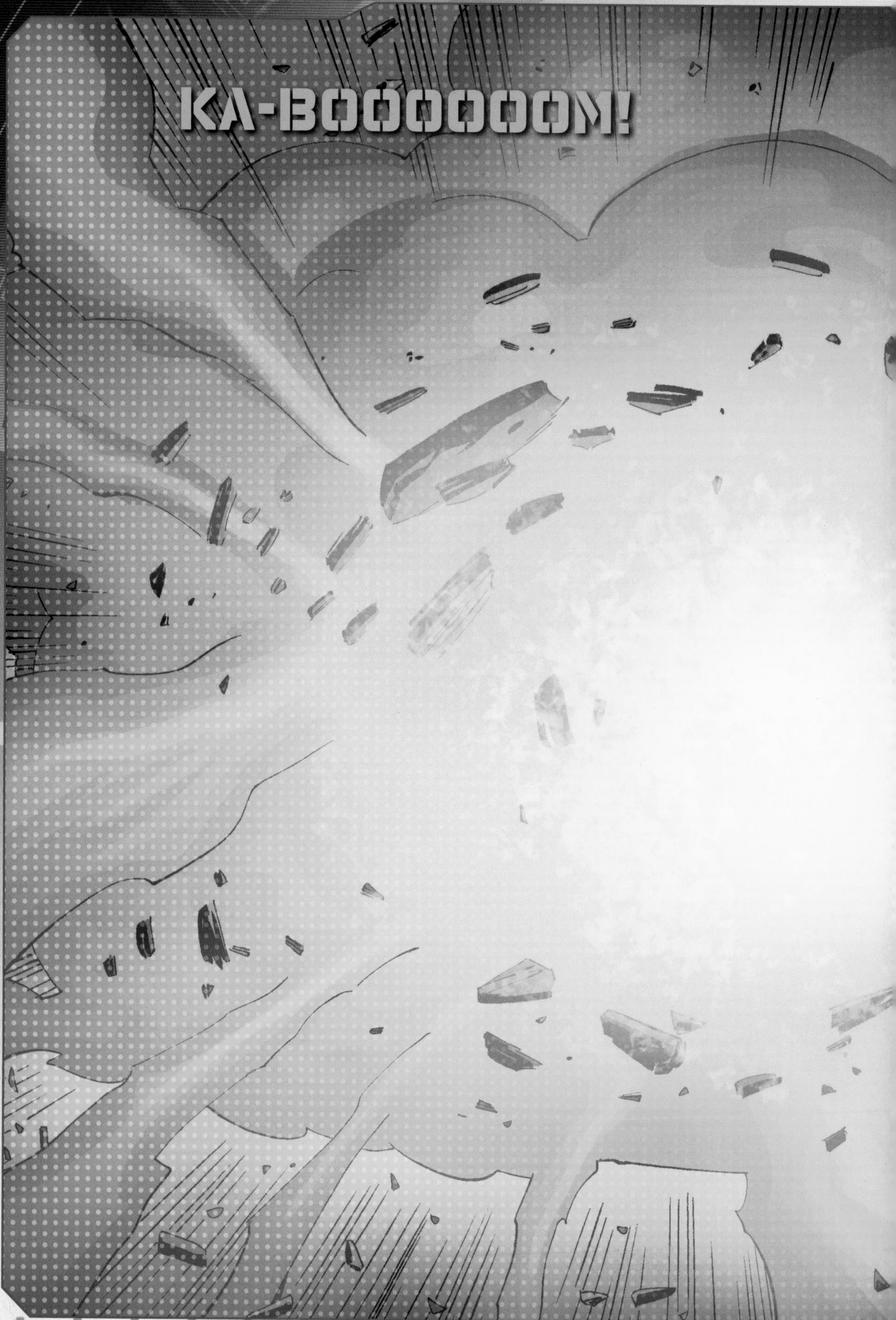
KA-BOOOOOOM!

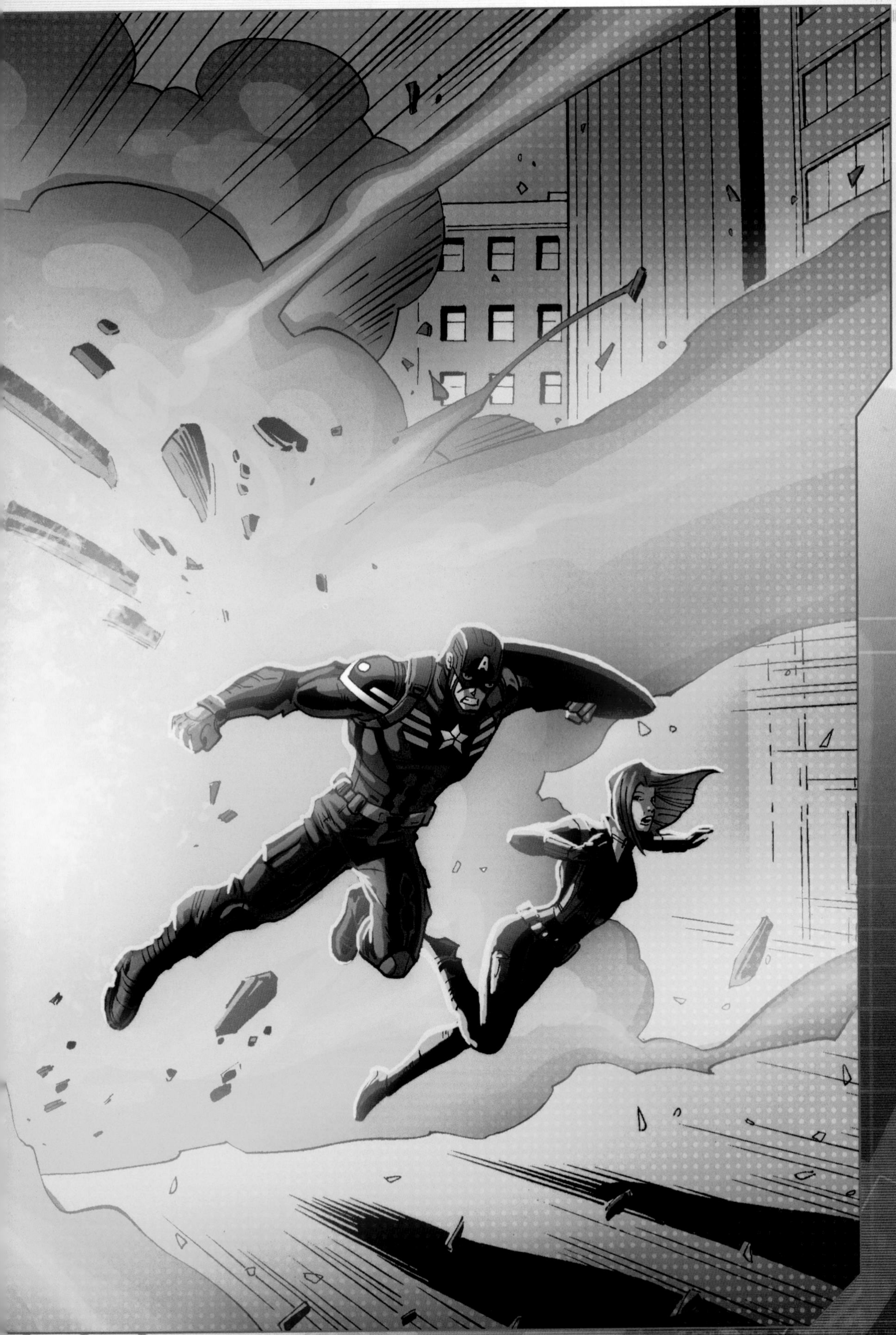

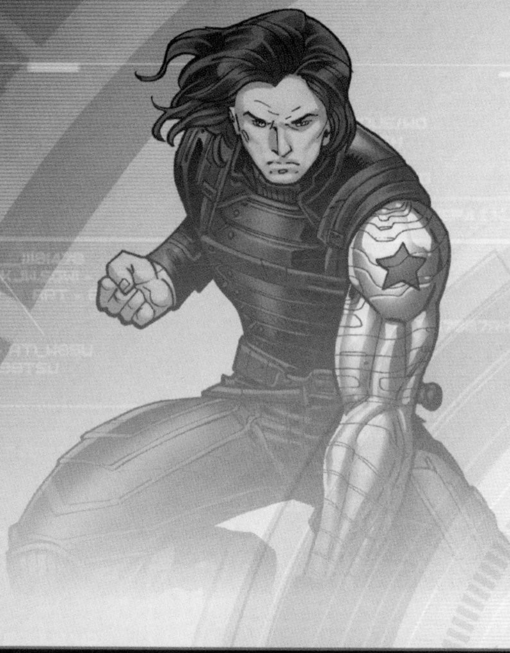

AS THE SMOKE CLEARED, STEVE SAW THAT BUCKY WAS GONE. Steve looked into the distance, slowly processing that his former best friend was now his worst enemy. He thought back to their childhood together, of how Bucky had supported him when Steve's mother died, how they'd fought side by side in World War II, and how Steve had thought he'd lost his best friend in combat. But now Bucky was back and was clearly not himself.

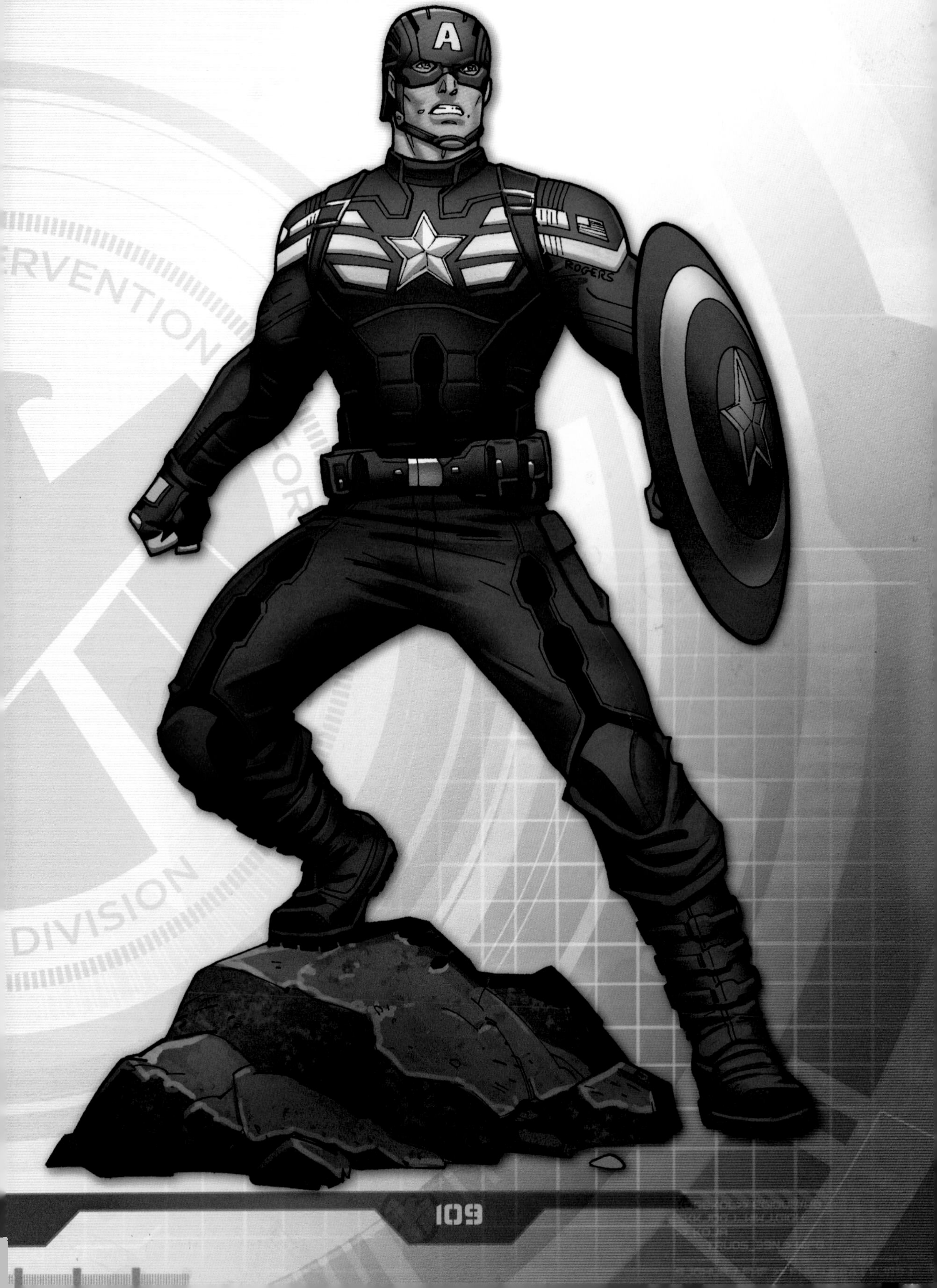
ROGERS

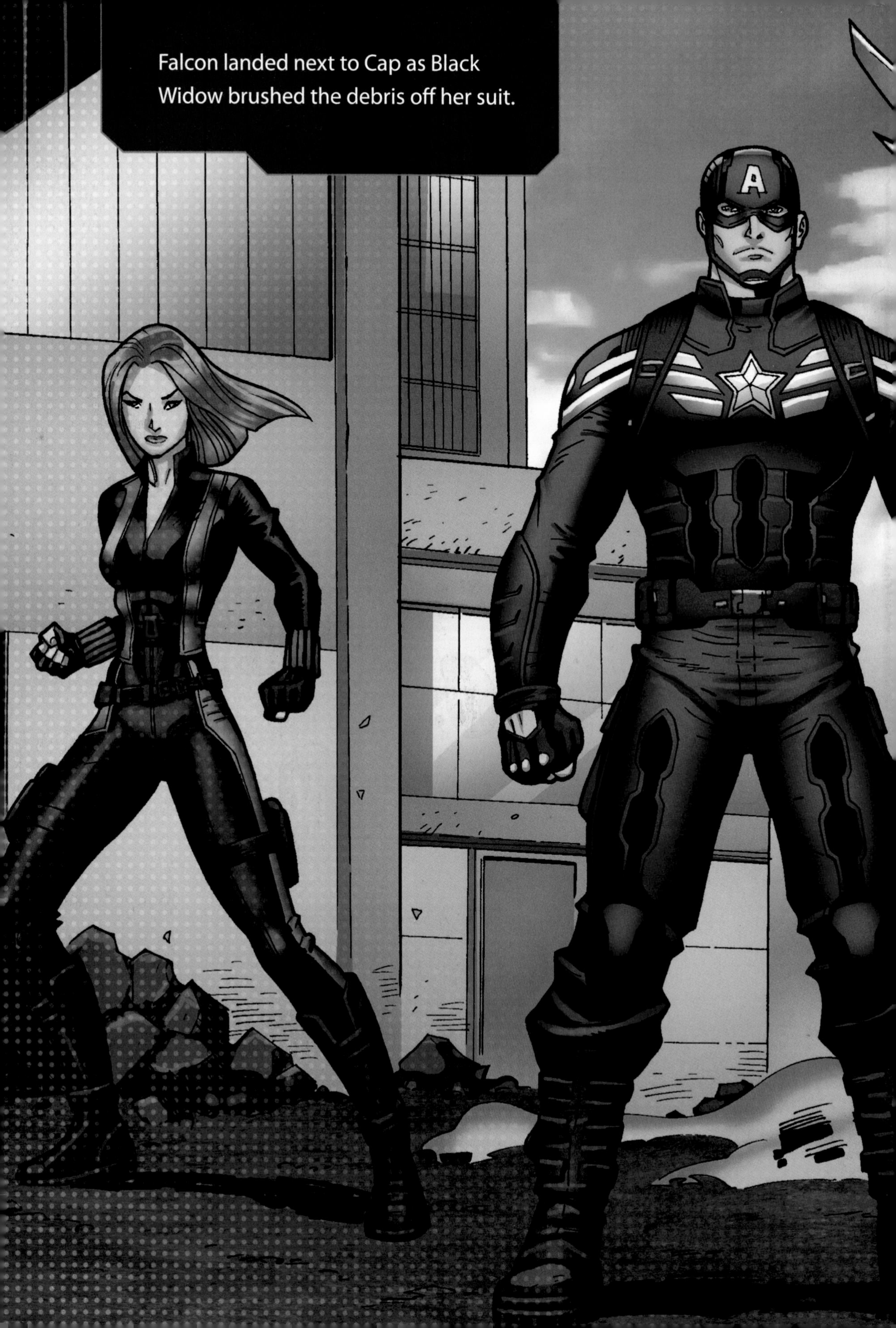
Falcon landed next to Cap as Black Widow brushed the debris off her suit.

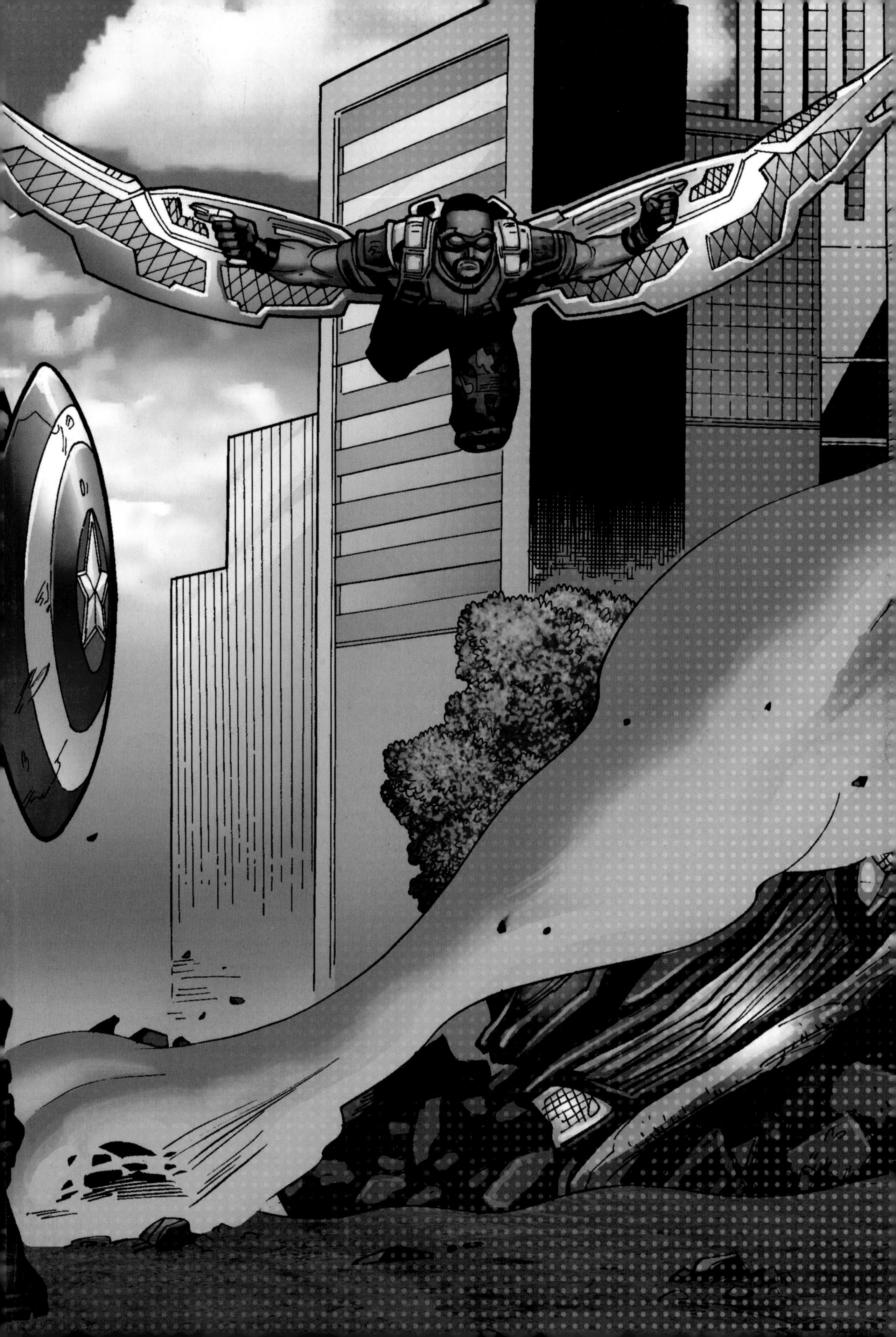

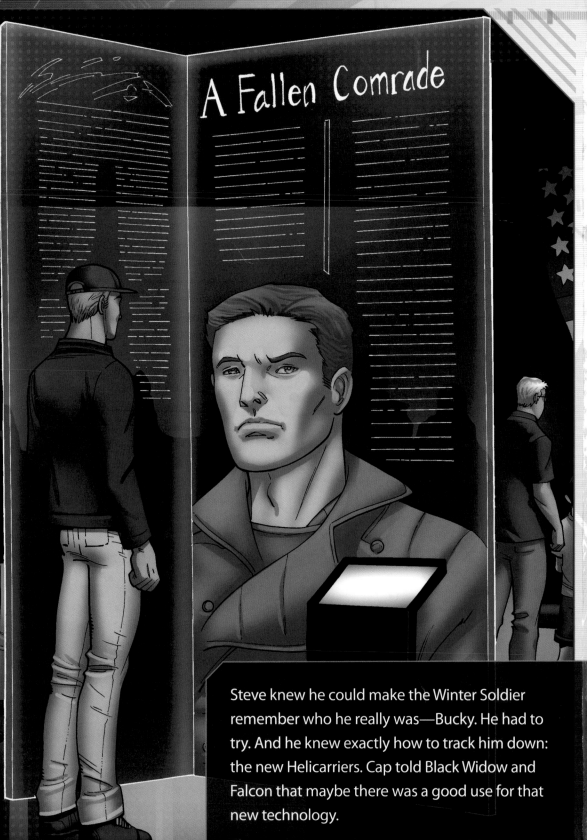

A Fallen Comrade

Steve knew he could make the Winter Soldier remember who he really was—Bucky. He had to try. And he knew exactly how to track him down: the new Helicarriers. Cap told Black Widow and Falcon that maybe there was a good use for that new technology.

There was no way Steve Rogers could rest until he and Bucky Barnes reunited as best friends— as they once had been and would be again.